The three of you make a beautiful family.

A knot formed in her throat. Ever since that stranger's comment, she'd had to battle the thrill it brought.

The baby whimpered.

Time to forget her silly emotions and take care of Abigail. And make dinner for Jake.

Pressing her cheek to Abigail's head, she inhaled her sweet smell. Longing tugged at her insides, and she had to tamp it back into the safe prison it had been in for years.

She'd just finished cooking and changed clothes when the front door opened.

"I'm home," Jake called, his deep voice sending her stomach flying as if she'd reached the highest point of a Ferris wheel.

Jake stepped into the kitchen…and whistled.

"I'm glad you appreciate a home-cooked meal."

His eyes swept her from head to toe. "I meant you, Violet. You look beautiful."

Born and raised in Kentucky, **Missy Tippens** met her very own hero when she headed to grad school in Atlanta, Georgia. She promptly fell in love and has lived in Georgia ever since. She and her pastor husband have been married for over twenty-five years and have been blessed with three children. After ten years of pursuing her publishing dream, Missy made her first sale to Love Inspired in 2007.

Books by Missy Tippens

Love Inspired

Her Unlikely Family
His Forever Love
A Forever Christmas
A Family for Faith
A House Full of Hope
Georgia Sweethearts
The Guy Next Door

The Doctor's Second Chance

Missy Tippens

Recycling programs
for this product may
not exist in your area.

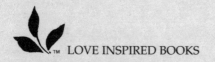

™ LOVE INSPIRED BOOKS

ISBN-13: 978-0-373-81835-8

The Doctor's Second Chance

Copyright © 2015 by Melissa L. Tippens

www.Harlequin.com

Printed in U.S.A.

And we know that all things work together for good to them that love God, to them who are the called according to his purpose.
—*Romans* 8:28

To the talented and dedicated physicians
who've cared for my children through the years.

To God, who is loving, patient and good.

Acknowledgments

Many thanks to my amazing
and generous Seekerville blog sisters
for helping me brainstorm this story!

Chapter One

Surely this isn't happening.

A baby, its tiny lips puckered, slept in a car seat at Jake West's feet. The child suddenly whimpered and jerked as if startled.

Jake's insides jerked in response.

He dragged his gaze back to his cousin with her hair in a messy ponytail and no makeup. His heart banged against his ribs. "You can't do this, Remy."

With red-rimmed eyes, she stared at the baby. Had she been crying or— "Are you high?"

She sighed. "No, I've been clean for a year."

"Then come on, don't be talking crazy."

"You owe me, Jake."

He'd heard those words the last time she'd popped into town—long enough to steal his wallet. "I don't owe you anything." His conscience pricked. Maybe he did. Maybe he was the whole reason for her problems.

A freebie diaper bag plastered with hospital and baby product logos slid down her shoulder. She plunked it on the floor, the gesture so final he flinched.

"You're not leaving that baby here with me," Jake said. "Take her to your parents."

"No, I want *you* to raise her, and I put a letter in her bag saying so."

A quick glance at Remy's stomach showed her as thin as ever. "You are her mother...aren't you?"

She nodded.

"And the father?"

"He died. No family." She drew in a stuttering breath. "All her papers are in the bag, including a medical consent form."

"Come on. Let's sit down and talk this out. You have other options."

One tear slid down her cheek, and she slapped it away, her expression remaining stony. "Don't you dare let her down." She glared at Jake, her eyes full of agony. "You're the responsible one, the good kid, remember?"

Words his aunt and uncle, who'd raised him, had always said about him as they'd measured their rebellious daughter against his be-good-so-they'll-keep-me behavior.

Remy reached out as if she wanted to touch her daughter but shoved her hands into the pockets of her wrinkled jeans instead, her gaze so full of longing it made Jake's chest hurt.

"Come on, let me fix you some dinner," he said, trying to sound friendly, upbeat. "I'll make your favorite. We'll talk."

"You can't make everything all better with a peanut butter and banana sandwich anymore, Jake. Now I need you to take care of *her*."

"Come on, Rem."

"Promise me."

"Remy."

"I mean it." Desperation flashed in her widened eyes. *"Promise."*

What could he do? Refuse? "I promise."

She turned and strode out the front door and down the steps toward an ancient beat-up sedan.

The hot July sun on the western horizon forced him to shield his eyes. "Where are you going?" he called. "You need help, Remy."

"I'll be fine. I'm just not mother material." She climbed in the car and started the engine.

Torn, he glanced back inside the house, afraid to leave the baby alone. He quickly went back to grab the carrier. By the time he made it outside, his cousin had peeled out of the driveway and sped down the street, too far away to catch the license plate number.

Tension in his neck sent throbbing pain to his head. With a palm mashed against his temple, he watched her vehicle slip into the distance.

He didn't know a thing about babies. He had a construction company to run. Had to be on site the next day. Not a place for infants.

Loud squalling dragged his attention back to the child, her chin quivering, fists and feet pumping.

Yes, there was a nearly newborn baby in his grasp. A baby he was now responsible for. And she was crying her little head off, turning wrinkled and red.

"Lord, help me." He headed back inside and set the carrier on the couch.

The little gal was buckled in some sort of car seat contraption with straps that looked like something from a race car. It took him a minute to figure out the harness. He finally worked her out of it and very carefully lifted her to his chest, gasping when he realized just how tiny she was. "You're no bigger than a minute."

She seemed so...*breakable*. As she cried, she rooted against his rough work shirt, dirty from the job site. He moved her to the crook of his arm, terrified he would lose his grip. *Like holding a football,* he reassured himself.

He rocked his arms a bit, and the crying stopped. She seemed to try to focus on his face, yet he wasn't even sure she could see him.

Such delicate features. And that head full of wispy black hair so much like Remy's made her seem even more vulnerable. His heart warmed.

But fear, yes, fear prevailed. What would he do with a little baby?

"I don't even know your name."

With a mewl, she scrunched up her face again. Was she in pain? Was all this crying normal?

His heart jammed up in his throat. He needed help. Someone to check her out to make sure she was okay. Someone to tell him what to do—at least until he could track down Remy to insist she come back and get the baby.

Surely Remy would come back to get her daughter.

Think, Jake. Calm down and think.

First, the baby needed to be checked by a doctor. But Jake's uncle, the town pediatrician, had recently sold the practice and was living in south Florida.

The new pediatrician? Jake hated to take his tiny charge to Violet Crenshaw. Just thinking her name made his blood pressure shoot up. The doctor had come in with her big-city lawyer, negotiating his uncle and aunt down to a rock-bottom price, practically stealing the struggling business from them at a time when they were worn down from dealing with Remy's problems and disappearance.

The baby's peeping threatened to turn to a wail. As he grabbed the diaper bag and dug through it looking for a bottle, his movements seemed to soothe her and stalled a full-blown fit.

Bouncing to keep her moving, he located several bottles. All empty. Then he discovered a can of formula. "Yes!" He shook it.

Powder?

The baby couldn't drink powder, so was Jake supposed to add water or milk? And did he need to boil it first? He twisted the can to read the label.

Another mewl sounded, and then she revved up like a band saw.

The little thing sure had a set of lungs on her.

Was something hurting her?

Shoving aside resentment of the new pediatrician, he returned the child to her car seat and quickly rebuckled her. Slinging the diaper bag over his shoulder, he headed to his truck.

He opened the back door of the crew cab, set the carrier on the seat and tried over and over to figure out where the seat belt was supposed to attach. The car seat appeared to be yard-sale quality, scratched and tattered, and if there had ever been instructions, they were worn off.

Doing the best he could, Jake got the seat strapped in and prayed for a safe drive.

As much as it galled him, he needed Violet Crenshaw's help. And badly.

Violet Crenshaw bid her assistant and receptionist goodbye and locked the door behind them. Then she stepped into her office, which was blessedly quiet, to enter figures into the computer. The tiny, utilitarian room hadn't been updated in years, probably decades. Rickety metal desk, worn-out computer chair, plain two-by-four wooden shelves spray-painted and set on brackets, boring beige walls. Violet's mother would have a conniption if she saw it. Would insist on calling in her favorite decorator to gut it and start fresh.

Of course, Violet's mother wouldn't see this office. Wouldn't see her cute rental home, either.

Pushing away old hurts, Violet clicked numbers into the computer. Until business picked up, she was stuck with the 1990s decor. And it was not picking up as she'd hoped.

Looking at the stack of bills, she let out a heavy sigh. The flailing practice had been a bargain, but attracting new patients was tough for an outsider in a small town. Especially when unfounded gossip abounded, fueled by the nephew of the beloved previous owners who'd said she'd supposedly *stolen* the business from them.

She had made an offer she could afford, and it had been accepted. According to her lawyer, she'd paid a fair price. She clung to the belief her good reputation would overcome the talk.

Word-of-mouth recommendations would take time, though. She hoped she could make it that long financially because she loved taking care of children and building relationships in a solo practice. Loved the small-town feel of Appleton, Georgia.

She shut down her computer. Time to head home. Maybe she'd make some pasta for dinner. She could watch a movie or—

What was that pounding sound?

Stepping into the hallway of the old house-turned-office, she listened. Someone was banging on the front door. She hurried to unlock and open it.

A burly man in dirty work clothes stood with his fist poised to knock again. "Oh, good, you're still here," he said.

Recognition dawned. "You!" She scrunched her nose at Jake West, the man who'd single-handedly tried to make her arrival in Appleton a living nightmare. "What do you want?"

His scruffy, bearded jaw twitched as if he was clenching his teeth. Bright blue eyes narrowed.

Well, good. She hoped her attitude aggravated him. He deserved it for all the aggravation he'd caused her.

He inclined his head toward his truck. "I need your help. A baby."

At the word *baby*, personal feelings fled, and she focused on the task at hand. Zipping over to the vehicle, she opened the door. "What's wrong?"

"I have no clue."

"Is she injured or sick?"

"I don't think so. She's crying a lot."

"I need more than that to go on." Incredulous, Violet jerked her gaze away from his wild-eyed baby blues. She unbuckled the seat belt from its unorthodox position and tried to untangle the car seat. "What on earth?"

"Let me get it," he sniped.

"Fine. Come inside." She marched ahead of him and waited, holding the door open.

He strode through the entryway, brushing against her, once again setting off her irritation.

"I'd heard you're single," she said. "When did you have a baby?"

He raised a brow. "I haven't birthed a baby lately. She belongs to my cousin. I'm…uh… babysitting."

Likely story, buddy. Probably some fling had landed him with this new *responsibility.* It would fit this rabble-rouser she'd had the displeasure of meeting.

"So why did you bring her to be seen?"

"I, uh…" He cleared his throat. "My cousin had to leave rather suddenly. I'd like to have the baby checked over to make sure she's okay. To get some instructions on caring for her."

Squinting, Violet gave him the once-over. "How do I know you didn't take this baby?"

Anger flashed in his eyes, eyes that had just turned ice-cold. "You know my family. We don't steal children."

Fine. Of course they didn't. But he was acting strangely. "Do you suspect the baby has been harmed or neglected?"

His steely gaze held hers, almost as if testing to see if she was trustworthy. "No. But since I don't have experience with kids, I'd feel better if you'd check her. I have signed medical consent."

Violet suspected there was a good bit more to this story of suddenly babysitting an infant who couldn't be more than a week or two old. "Of course. Bring her back to an exam room."

She turned on lights as she went. "Next time, please make an appointment."

"Will do, if I have more than five minutes' notice."

As soon as Jake set the carrier on the examination table, the baby started to fuss.

Violet lifted her out of the seat, and the little one began to root against her chest. "Hungry, are we? Well, I'm sure your cousin Jake will get you a bottle ready while I weigh you."

Jake froze, eyes wide, as if she'd blinded him with her otoscope.

"You do have a bottle for her, don't you?"

He reached inside the diaper bag and pulled out a can. "There's this powdery formula. And bottles."

He sounded clueless. How would this child survive? How had his cousin dared leave the baby with *him*?

Violet huffed. "Go down the hall. There are samples of that exact brand in the storage closet on the right."

"Yeah. I know where the sample closet is."

Of course he did. He'd probably spent time in his aunt and uncle's office.

While he was gone, she weighed and measured the baby girl, jotting the figures on the paper covering the exam table. "I'll need to make her a file," she called. "And I need that medical consent form. Do you happen to have any of her records with you?"

He lumbered into the room holding up a disposable, formula-filled bottle, smiling as if he'd discovered precious gold. "Yes, in her bag. I'll find them."

"What's her name?"

With his back to her, he ignored the question and seemed to frantically search, tossing out diapers and wipes, empty bottles and clothes. At the bottom of the bag, he found a folder. "Here it is."

She broke the seal off the bottle, popped the top and began to feed the hungry baby, who slurped down the food. As Jake flipped through the records, Violet headed to grab another bottle to send home with him.

Sweet blue eyes stared up at her before finally turning sleepy. Violet's chest tightened.

Holding and feeding a precious baby never failed to open up old wounds, renewing the pain of having her own baby taken from her and put up for adoption by her parents.

Yet the opportunity reminded her that there were many children around town who needed a caring touch. Needed someone to look out for them.

"She's falling asleep." Violet put the baby to her shoulder and patted her back. "Be sure you always burp her like this after you feed her."

Once the baby belched, she returned her to the exam table. "I'll do a quick check and then she can have a nap in her car seat."

Violet glanced at Jake. He was watching every move she made, his eyes taking it all in like a first-time parent overwhelmed by a new life depending on him, afraid he'd do something wrong. She couldn't help but smile as she examined the baby's ears. "You never told me her name."

Jake's brain nearly buzzed. How could he tell this doctor that he had no idea what the child's name was? A child in *his* care.

He and Dr. Crenshaw were already adversarial. And now he was going to have to admit he had no contact information for the mother. No baby name. No father's name. No mother's address. Nothing but a copy of hospital records from Atlanta labeled *Baby Girl West*. He assumed Remy had filled out a birth certificate application, so surely the girl had a legal name.

What about those papers she mentioned?

One last, frantic flip through the documents in the bag revealed a folded copy of the birth certificate paperwork crammed between two folders along with the medical consent to treat form. When he read the name on the form, Jake sucked in a breath.

Remy had named the girl after his mother.

"Abigail," he choked out. "Her name's Abigail."

As the doctor continued the exam, Jake wondered at Remy's intentions for the girl. Had she planned all along for Jake to raise Abigail? Or had the decision been sudden, born out of desperation?

"Ears look good." Violet warmed the stethoscope and listened to the baby's chest and back. "Heartbeat and lungs are perfect."

With her short, wavy black hair, cut so that it flipped some at the ends, Violet looked too young to be a doctor. But despite the hair, her big, serious hazel eyes and white lab coat made her a convincing professional.

She glanced at the baby's belly and poked around. "Umbilical cord has already fallen off. Healed nicely. She seems to be in good health."

Relief swept through him. At least Remy had been taking good care of her.

"What's her birth date?"

That info he did have. "She was born on the Fourth of July."

Dr. Crenshaw pulled a sheet of paper out of a file folder and charted the weight on a graph. "Two weeks old. She's at the fiftieth percentile. Weight, length and head circumference look good. And I also need her last name." She smiled, but it didn't reach her eyes. Instead, frustration seemed to spark at his inability to focus and communicate basic facts.

The baby looked groggy, her belly full, content. His earlier panic inched down a notch. "Abigail West." He glanced again at the form, his chest tightening. Remy had given the girl his dad's middle name—which was also Jake's middle name. "Abigail Lee, L-e-e, West."

"Thank you," the pediatrician mumbled, her tone adding an unspoken *finally* as she filled in the blanks on some sort of form.

She probably questioned his mental faculties. He was beginning to wonder himself. "Here's that medical release form from her mother. Do you have some kind of booklet on basic infant care? I wasn't sure about whether to boil the water or use milk for the formula. Or how to sterilize the bottles—or if I even need to. That kind of thing."

"Don't give her cow's milk yet. Here." She wrapped the baby up like a burrito and leaned close to set her in his arms. As she did, the doc's short, flippy black hair caught on his beard and tickled his chin.

"I'll go make Abigail's file," she said. "You should probably change her diaper so she'll take a nice long nap for you."

Diapers. There would be lots of messy diapers in his near future. The thought nearly made him wretch.

"You have changed her diaper, haven't you?"

"No."

"Ever changed *any* diaper?"

"No." His incompetence had been revealed. Could she report someone for being an inept babysitter?

She simply sighed. "Sounds like you need a crash course."

"I do. Would you be willing to come home with me to help get Abigail settled? I'll pay you whatever you'd bill for, what? Four appointments in an hour? Six?"

"Do you have a friend you could ask?" Her hazel eyes were serious, concerned, as if she feared he didn't have any friends. Which only showed she must think the worst of him. Still, for some reason, he found the concern endearing.

Caution, Jake. No matter how cute she looks with her feathery hair and big serious eyes, this conniving woman took advantage of Aunt Edith and Uncle Paul. "No, I don't have anyone else to ask. The older ladies in my church may not know the current child-rearing recommendations. I don't know the young moms well enough to ask a favor. And the women I've dated...well, none of them would be good with kids."

She gave a derisive snort. "Not dating the maternal type, huh?"

No, his dates were more into skydiving or mountain climbing than children. But he wasn't going to stoop to answer her snooty question. She could think badly of him all she wanted. He didn't value her opinion unless it had to do with Abigail. "I'll pay you. Just name your price."

"My price? Quit bad-mouthing me to people in town."

Stunned by her bluntness, he huffed. "I've only spoken the truth."

"There's no way you know every detail of the contract negotiations. Get the facts straight before you start smearing someone's reputation."

Oh, he knew all about the contract negotiations between her and Paul and Edith—and how she'd found fault with the way the business had been run, had brought in her expensive Atlanta lawyer to do her bidding. Jake even knew the final sale price—which he thought entirely too low for something his aunt and uncle had built for decades, since before Jake's parents died.

Looking around the room at the same child-friendly posters and colorful furniture his aunt and uncle had lovingly put in place made him sad. Jake wouldn't back down, wouldn't let the doctor from the huge city clinic come in acting as if his family were bumpkins, and taking advantage of them, without repercussions.

Despite his opinion of her, though, he needed her help. For the baby's sake. "Will you please help me with Abigail?" The words grated in his throat, nearly choking him.

She stared into his eyes until the moment became uncomfortable. Briefly, he thought he saw pain, but then the pediatrician snatched a diaper out of the bag. "Helping you set up for a baby is not something I can bill as a medical service."

"I'll pay you directly, like a babysitting subcontractor."

"I'll give you an hour."

The tension in his shoulders relaxed as he laid Abigail on the exam table. "Thank you."

Violet made quick work of the diaper, so smoothly the little gal barely stirred from her sleep. "I'll teach you to do this on her next diaper change."

Once she was done, she handed the baby back to him. He gently buckled her into her car seat, even managing not to wake her. Maybe he'd get the hang of this temporary fatherhood job after all.

As he lifted the carrier, Abigail suddenly cried out as if in some sort of pain.

"Did your cousin happen to mention the baby being colicky?" the doc asked over the screeching cries.

He swung the car seat back and forth, trying to soothe her. "No."

"This might be a long few nights for you, Jake."

Few nights? If only...

"That diaper bag is all I have," he said. "I guess I need to stop and buy some supplies on the way home."

"I don't mind picking up the basics for you before I come over."

"But—"

"You can pay me back later."

Before he could refuse, she said, "I heard you moved into your aunt and uncle's house. I'll be there shortly." She was no-nonsense, used to being obeyed. She breezed out of the room, presumably to show him out.

When they reached the front door, she unlocked it and held it open.

"I appreciate it." With a nod, he headed out, his tiny second cousin or cousin-once-removed or whatever she was to him blasting his ears.

"Come on now, Abigail," he cooed in his best soothing voice, a tone he didn't even know he could make.

He lifted her carrier to the truck's backseat. Once again, he struggled to buckle the car seat in place.

"How about I show you how to do that?" Violet said from behind him.

When he agreed, she made her way between him and the truck, spun the car seat around backward and scooted it to the middle seat belt. "Infants this age must be rear-facing. And there's supposed to be a base that stays in your vehicle that the seat latches into. Until you buy a new one, which I recommend, the strap goes through here." She pointed to a slot on the back. With the seat facing the correct direction, the seat belt easily slipped through and locked Abigail in place.

"Now that makes perfect sense," he said with a laugh. "Should have thought of it myself."

Violet turned and faced him, looking satisfied. She was so close the evening sun reflected off flecks of gold in her eyes.

He stepped back, allowing her to slip past him. She did so quickly and darted toward the office building, as if anxious to get away.

He felt almost guilty for the things he'd thought and said about her. Almost. "Thank you, Dr. Crenshaw. I know you didn't have to do all this, to go the extra mile."

She stiffened as if surprised and glanced at

him over her shoulder. "My purpose in life is to help children, Mr. West."

Of course she wasn't acting out of kindness toward him. But he could live with that.

With a nod, she stepped inside and shut the door.

Hoping the sound of the engine might help lull Abigail to sleep, Jake hopped in and started the truck. By the time he'd driven halfway home, she had quieted.

Thank You, Lord.

Now, if You'd just help me find a way not to alienate the doc before Remy gets back, I'd be doubly grateful.

Chapter Two

Violet walked up to the front door of the cute, brick Craftsman-style bungalow with its perfectly landscaped and manicured lawn. The West home backed up to her tiny rental house. Literally. Nothing but a low row of hedges separated their backyards.

The huge front porch with a swing and window boxes cascading with petunias invited her to come sit a while. Exactly the feeling she'd dreamed about having in a small town. If only she could find time to make some friends.

Holding three bags of newborn necessities in her left hand, she rapped on the door with the other. Time to show this clueless man how to take care of his baby cousin.

Jake opened the door, his broad shoulders and husky physique filling the space, making her stomach flutter.

No, no fluttering allowed.

"Hey, come on in," he said as he reached for the bags with strong arms. "Let me take those."

He appeared to be six-one or six-two, maybe two hundred twenty-five pounds. A large man, built of solid muscle without a pinch of fat.

"Thanks, but, uh…" *Focus.* "There's more in the car. I left it open for you."

"Got it. You can head on back to the kitchen."

She stepped inside and passed through a well-used living room fitted with older, broken-in furniture. Abigail slept soundly in her carrier on the worn tweed couch. Violet kept going until she found the kitchen and then began to unload the bags.

The outdated furnishings, which must have belonged to Edith and Paul West, lent a homey feel, something her parents' home had lacked because her mother hired a decorator to redo the house every few years.

A small, drop-leaf breakfast table by the window, however, looked new. On it sat an opened newspaper beside a laptop computer. Discarded after breakfast or when his cousin showed up needing a babysitter?

Other than the newspaper, everything was in its place, neat as a pin, and wasn't at all what she would picture for a busy bachelor. Surprisingly, the rooms felt welcoming.

For some reason, the tidy, cozy home didn't fit with Jake's overgrown, wavy brown hair, closely trimmed beard and rugged, mountain-man looks.

Shaking her head, she laughed. What had she expected? A tent and camping stove?

"Disposable diapers," he declared as he entered the room and plopped the bags on the counter. "Lots of diapers. Enough to single-handedly overload the county landfill."

"Abigail will use all of those in about a week."

"No kidding?" He tucked all but one of the packs in the pantry. "Guess I need to practice changing her, but I hate to wake her."

"We can work on the feeding first."

She pointed to a case of already-prepared formula. "I figured you'd rather splurge on ready-to-feed formula instead of having to mix the powder."

"Good call."

She held up a carton and gave instructions on how to heat it.

He pulled bottles out of the diaper bag. "These are the ones Remy sent."

Examining their condition, Violet wrinkled her nose. One was coated with the curdling remnants of formula. The nipples looked worn. Too worn, as if Remy had gotten them as hand-me-downs. "You know, I think since you don't know where these have been, we'll boil them first. And we can throw some of them away. I bought a few new ones."

His expression hardened. "My cousin may not have the best of everything, but I don't think she would expose her baby to unsanitary conditions."

Spoken as if he thought Violet was used to having the best of everything. The fact he must think her haughty nipped at her conscience. How many times had she been mortified by her mother's snobbish actions? She'd vowed never to have that same attitude.

"I'm sorry. I didn't mean to offend. But nipples do wear out and tear, which could choke the baby. We have to be careful."

With tense shoulders easing, he let out a breath. "Okay."

"We also need to boil the new bottles and nipples before the first use. Do you have a large soup pot we can use?"

He opened cabinet after cabinet, searching. The man was obviously a bachelor because the shelves were mostly empty.

"Found this." He pulled out a pan that was big enough to heat a can of soup.

"You don't cook, huh?"

"I know how, but I'm not here much. I make sandwiches for lunch and give Edna a lot of business at the diner."

"I'm glad I brought you a case of sample bottles to get you through until you can buy a larger pan." She couldn't help but wonder at how much sense his cousin, Remy, had to leave a baby here.

Pulling out an informational brochure she'd brought with her, she showed him how to clean bottles with the brush she'd purchased and how to use the dishwasher for future washings. He seemed to be taking in all the information and even jotted notes.

Satisfied, she pulled out the baby monitor she'd picked up at the hardware store. "Now, you'll need this so you'll hear Abigail when she cries during the night."

The wary look on his face was comical. He had no idea how his life was about to change.

"I guess she needs a room. And a crib."

Violet's stomach sank. "You mean you don't have a place for her to sleep?"

"Well, there are two extra bedrooms," he sputtered, looking offended. "I had no notice about Remy dropping off the baby."

She wouldn't ask more questions and risk him getting his back up. "Don't put her in your bed. Just remove the comforter, pillows and blankets and put her on the guest bed for tonight. Tomorrow, you can buy a crib. Since it's short-term, a portable one will be fine."

At his look of further confusion, she let out a sigh. "Can I use your computer? I'll show you the items you'll probably need to buy."

He pointed her toward the table. "Good idea.

Will you listen for Abigail while I go change out of my work clothes?"

"Sure."

While he banged around in a nearby bedroom, Violet carried the laptop to the living room, where the baby was sleeping. She pulled up the website for a local discount store and put a fairly long list of items in the shopping cart.

Down the hallway, water ran for a few minutes. Before long, Jake showed up with wet hair and wearing jeans and a cottony soft T-shirt, smelling clean and way too appealing.

She popped up off the couch. Handed over the laptop. "Here, I put some things in your shopping cart. Figured you could print and take it with you to the store tomorrow. Travel bed, sheets, portable changing station, more bottles, diaper disposal system, baby bath tub and bathing essentials."

His face scrunched in disgust. "Diaper disposal system?"

"Yes. To help with odors."

"Oh, man." He raked a hand through his hair, leaving brown strands standing up. "How am I going to bathe her? I've never even seen someone do that."

She fought the urge to smooth his disheveled hair back into place. "You'll figure it out. Watch a YouTube video or something." She glanced at her watch. "Well, my hour will be up soon, and I haven't had a chance to show you how to change a diaper."

"Deserting me already?" He laughed, but she could see worry in the squint of his eyes and crease in his forehead.

"That was our agreement." She picked up the diaper bag and looked inside. "Is this everything Remy left with you?"

"It is."

Violet pulled out a receiving blanket. "I'll show you how to swaddle her so she feels more secure. Once you purchase a crib, always lay her on her back to sleep. And never put anything else in the crib with her."

His cell phone rang as he nodded. "I've got to take this call. It's work." Striding toward to the kitchen, his deep voice carried to the living room. He was not happy. Something about a load of floor tile not being delivered as promised.

"No, that's unacceptable," Jake said. "I want it there tomorrow morning by nine."

Abigail woke and began to fuss. Violet took her out of her seat. "Hey, sweet girl. Jake's busy right now, so it's just you and me." The baby was warm and had that wonderful baby shampoo smell. However, her diaper weighed a ton.

The phone conversation ended and footsteps sounded on the hardwood floor.

"Okay, girlfriend," Violet said to Abigail. "I

have to warn you. It's time for Jake's first ever diaper change. Cut him some slack, okay?"

When she looked up, Jake stood in the doorway, a half smile on his face. "No need to warn her of my ineptitude. She'll know soon enough."

Though he was kidding, there was an edge of truth in what he said. He truly was in over his head.

Unfortunately, he might not fare well, and she worried about Abigail. Maybe she should check in on her tomorrow.

No, that wasn't her place. It wasn't as if Remy or Jake was a personal friend.

Once Violet set up a makeshift diaper-changing area on the dresser, she showed Jake how to clean Abigail, slip a disposable diaper under her bottom and fasten it. Then she had him give it a try.

The first attempt left him chuckling. Despite Violet covering her mouth, a laugh slipped out.

He truly was pathetic at diapering.

"How's that?" he asked after his second attempt. The diaper was mostly straight but was extremely loose.

Looking into his hopeful eyes, she felt a thread of connection that gave the tiniest of tugs on her heart. She could not afford a thread of anything with this man who claimed she was a shady person and felt free to share that opinion around town.

"I'm afraid that will leak," she said, refocusing on the task at hand. "Try to fasten it tighter. It won't hurt her or cut off her circulation. It's stretchy."

Biting his lip while concentrating, he jumped in once again like a good student, determined to succeed. But this time Abigail started to fuss. "Uh-oh. I'll never manage this with her wiggling."

"She'll always wiggle, so you may as well learn to deal with it."

"Man, the doc is harsh," he mumbled into the baby's ear.

Violet caught herself smiling. "Hey, I can show you harsh by walking out right now."

"I take it back. Now…I'm trying again." Once, twice, he made the diaper too loose. The third time, he sighed. "This one's too tight."

"Wait." Violet ran a finger along the waist and leg holes, checking. "That's perfect. You did it!" She applauded him before she thought better of it, but then reined in her excitement, her face heating.

"Now who's inept?" Jake grinned, eyes gleaming with victory. "I'll be teaching a parenting class before you know it."

At his proud look and touch of humor, her breath gave a little hitch. She should *not* let his funny side affect her.

"Nice job," she said as she checked her watch.

"Oh, look. My hour is up. I jotted a suggested feeding schedule and left it on your kitchen counter. Call my assistant tomorrow if you have questions."

In other words, don't call me.

"Time's up already?" He carefully tucked Abigail in the crook of his arm, becoming a regular pro at carrying her.

Violet had always had a weakness for a big strong man holding a baby. How different might her life have been if she'd fallen for someone strong and responsible all those years ago?

"The receipt for the baby items is also on the kitchen counter," Violet said. "You can mail a check to my office."

"What's your charge for the hour of training?"

Lifting her chin, she focused on Abigail. "Don't worry about it."

"No, I insist."

"Consider it a favor for a new patient."

His brows drew downward, and he looked uncomfortable. "We had an agreement. It's been worth every penny I owe you."

She couldn't bring herself to ask for money for doing a task she had enjoyed. Besides, it would only add to his image of her being mercenary. "Instead, make a donation to your favorite charity for children."

"That's generous of you."

Her heart raced as hope shot through her.

Hope that maybe he would believe she hadn't ripped off his aunt and uncle and that she was a decent person.

She grabbed her purse and headed toward the front door.

Close on her heels, he followed. "I'll mail you a check tomorrow. Thank you for buying the baby stuff and for coming over. I owe you a favor."

She could imagine how it pained him to say that. "You don't owe me anything. I like to think I can make a difference in the community. Like your aunt and uncle did."

He nodded but didn't comment. She couldn't help but wonder if he considered her a poor substitute. Sure, they hadn't known how to run a business well. But they'd taken good care of the local children for a long time, had been loved by the Appleton residents.

Would she ever feel as if she had a place in the town?

"I guess I'll see you around, Dr. Crenshaw," he said.

"Yes, and if Abigail is still in town in two weeks, be sure to schedule an appointment for her next vaccination."

"Oh, I'm sure Remy will take care of that."

"Well, good night. I hope you get some sleep."

She truly did hope he had a good night. For Abigail's sake. Yet she couldn't help but worry about the tiny, dependent girl. How would she fare with this man who had absolutely no experience dealing with infants?

The insecurity on Jake's face, as well as the fact Abigail looked so vulnerable in his arms, made Violet's decision.

To ease her mind and ensure the baby was thriving, she would check on Abigail over the weekend.

Jake sat in his truck Saturday morning rubbing red, scratchy eyes and trying to read the directions for the soft baby carrier he'd bought first thing that morning as he'd learned his way around the baby section of the local discount store. Abigail had spared him and slept in the cart through the whole shopping trip.

Probably because she'd cried late into the night.

After nearly four hours of inconsolable crying, he'd looked up colic on the internet and thought that must be what she had because she didn't seem sick otherwise. Still, if she had another night like the last, he'd take her to the doctor to be on the safe side.

With the fabric carrier assembled, adjusted to fit and strapped on him, Jake climbed in the backseat and lifted Abigail from her car seat. Then he followed the step-by-step, very complicated directions for slipping her into the fabric that would hold her against his chest, kind of like a reverse backpack.

As he was hooking one of the head supports, her little body slipped sideways, about stopping his heart. He quickly stabilized her head and snapped the buckle into place. Assured she was peacefully snoozing and wouldn't fall out of the contraption, he climbed out of the truck, hoping he could work awhile.

His flooring subcontractor, Zeb, a trim man in his sixties wearing jeans and an old blue work shirt, stood at the front of the brick ranch home they were building with his arms crossed, waiting.

"Hey, Zeb. Sorry again about the tile delivery. Pete assured me he'd have it here by nine this morning."

"We can't finish as promised if he doesn't. I've already lost a day." Zeb's eyes narrowed as he spotted a tiny head peeking out of the carrier contraption. "Uh, congratulations?"

"She belongs to Remy. I'm babysitting."

A big breath of air whooshed out of him. "That's good. Was afraid I'd missed something big."

Jake pressed fingers against his burning eyes. "Had a rough night. She cried for hours."

"Lots of prayer going on in the West household, huh?"

"You know it. More like begging for mercy." He laughed. "You know anything about colic?"

"Can't say that I do." Zeb squinted into the late-morning sun. "Except I remember one of my girls had luck by changing her baby's formula."

Jake nodded. Zeb had kids and grandkids, so Jake could trust parenting tips from the man. "Have you been inside? Did my cabinets get delivered?"

"Not yet. The guys are still taping and muddin' drywall and priming."

Jake needed to go inside, make sure everyone was on schedule and the work met his expectations. But a work site wasn't the place for a baby. "If Pete isn't here in fifteen minutes, I'll call him."

"Thanks, Jake. We'll do a good job for you."

"You always do." He only hired top-notch subcontractors, and Zeb and his crew were the best around.

Jake made a phone call, and as soon as he hung up, Abigail began to stir. She'd be hungry when she woke. She'd also need a fresh diaper... or two or twenty.

There was no way he'd be able to work while caring for a baby. He needed to find child care, and quickly.

Turning to go to the truck, he spotted Violet's shiny, older model luxury convertible pulling in behind his vehicle. She'd either had it for several years or had bought it used. Either way, he had to admit she might have a good head on her shoulders. Well, except for the brand-new, very expensive tires.

"Oh, hello," she said as she climbed out.

"Hey." Had she been out for a Saturday drive and just happened to spot him? Or had she come to check up on Abigail?

The latter was the more likely scenario.

Wearing shorts and a flowery pink top, Violet looked like a breath of fresh air. Her mile-long, shapely legs caught the attention of a few of his men watching from the garage area.

Jake put himself between them and Violet, blocking their view. "I was just headed to change Abigail and get a bottle."

"Don't let me stop you."

Would Violet hang around? Jake had parked in the shade and planned to change Abigail's diaper right there in the truck. Violet better not breathe down his neck and complain about his decision. He had to do a decent job with the diaper, though, or else Abigail would be strapped to his chest, a loaded weapon ready to wreak havoc.

By the time he'd laid the baby on a changing pad placed on the vehicle seat, she was fully awake.

Violet peeked around his shoulder. "Looks like that diaper's on pretty good."

"Yep."

"So I guess you don't need any help with the clean one."

"Nope." He successfully changed her despite the tense woman watching. When Abigail fussed, he popped a bottle in her mouth and tucked her in the crook of his arm.

"How did she sleep last night?"

"Not well. I'll bring her by the office if we continue to have problems."

"Problems? What type of problems?" Violet asked, going from the diaper police back to pediatrician.

"She cried from eight until nearly midnight. I think she has colic."

"Well, there are several things you can try, like—"

"Thanks, but I read about it on the internet. Got some ideas." He nodded toward town. "And I bought your whole list of baby stuff, so we're good to go."

The Pete's Flooring truck arrived with the tile as Abigail slurped down the formula.

"Excuse me a minute." Jake strode across the lot.

Happy and bright-eyed, Abigail let the nipple slip out of her mouth. He tucked the bottle in his front pants pocket. Abigail watched him as he directed Pete where to drop off the tile. While Pete's men unloaded the pallets, the truck with the kitchen cabinets arrived.

"Jake, do you want me to hold her?" Violet called as she picked her way across the muddy expanse of the future front lawn.

"Hang on just a minute."

Needing to direct the second delivery, and hoping to prove to the doc that he could take care of his baby cousin, Jake safely tucked Abigail in the carrier against his chest, talking sweetly to her in a voice that no longer felt strange. A couple of his men snickered.

Ignoring them, he pointed the second group of deliverymen toward the garage. Once they finished unloading, they started backing out, nearing Pete's truck.

"Whoa!" Jake rushed over, waving his arms to stop the collision.

Startled by his voice and sudden movement, Abigail shrieked, her arms and legs flailing. He quickly soothed her, patting and cooing.

Jake finally sent the cabinet truck on its way, then turned and found Violet standing at the front of the house watching him. Frowning.

She glared at the mess of scraps and tools around them. "This isn't an appropriate place for a two-week-old baby. You're going to have to make other arrangements or—" She huffed.

Or what? he wanted to say but didn't dare

challenge her in the situation. He'd already come to the same conclusion himself.

"This isn't a normal day," he said instead. "I'm still juggling, trying to figure out my new schedule with Abigail. I just dropped by to check on the tile delivery." Mainly, he needed to get through his first full day with a baby.

Today, on four and a half hours of sleep, he'd bought baby equipment and supplies, changed several diapers, fed her two bottles and coaxed three burps. He'd even managed to keep Abigail alive. That victory must count for something.

He probably deserved a medal.

Violet stood looking at him as if he was a nail in one of her four-hundred-dollar tires.

He walked away before he said something rude.

Close on his heels, she followed, her spotless white flip-flops getting mired in mud. He stopped and turned.

Looking at her feet, she didn't notice his sudden change in direction and barreled into him. Slowly, she looked up, frustration flashing in her pretty eyes. "This place is too hazardous for a baby."

"You're more at risk in your open-toed shoes than a baby is tucked against my chest." The chest Violet stood literally six inches from. "So did you come just to see if I had Abigail with me?"

"I happened to be out. Saw your truck. Thought I'd stop by and see if she needs anything."

He narrowed his eyes. "More likely, you wanted to make sure she survived the night."

She jammed her hands on her khaki-clad hips, a perfect warrior pose, cheeks bright red, sparks of fury in her brownish-green eyes. "Okay, you want the brutal truth? I doubt you're prepared to take care of a baby this young."

"Ah, so you're capable of honesty after all. Who would've guessed?"

"At least I'm not being nasty, judging you on something I know nothing about."

Zeb stepped around the corner of the house to see what the commotion was about. Jake waved him off. He didn't need the man asking questions about him and the new pediatrician.

Violet didn't flinch at the interruption. Didn't seem to care they had an audience. She glared at him, ready to battle it out.

He wouldn't back down, either. "Abigail is fine. Check her out if you want."

The offer knocked her back a step. With an irritated huff, she peeked at the baby. "I see you bought a carrier. And you appear to have it attached correctly."

"I can read directions, you know."

She worked her hands around the edges of the fabric, feeling for all Abigail's body parts.

"You seem to have her in a good position. She looks comfortable."

Dr. Crenshaw was so close her hair brushed his chin again. Though he'd expect her to smell like a doctor's office—of sick people and disinfectant—she actually smelled good, like flowers mixed with something fresh and clean.

When she looked up, her eyes met his and widened. The tiny flecks of light gold around her pupils made her look young, vulnerable.

But Violet Crenshaw was not some delicate creature. Hadn't she just proven it by charging into his job site with both barrels loaded?

She cleared her throat and stepped away.

What had made her change from last night, when she'd been helpful? Was it all because he'd yelled to stop a collision and made Abigail cry? He stepped around Violet to head to the truck. "See you around, Doc."

She looked annoyed that he'd cut her off. But he'd had enough. Tomorrow at church he would find someone else who could help him. Preferably someone who had experience with a colicky child. Someone who didn't have gorgeous legs, who didn't look at him all innocent and vulnerable, twisting his insides into a knot.

Thankfully, the pediatrician didn't go to Jake's church. If all went well with Abigail, he wouldn't have to see Violet again before Remy returned.

* * *

What in the world am I doing?

Meddling.

But that wasn't the whole truth. She was also there as the result of a nudge from her conscience…or maybe from God?

Violet drew in a slow, deep breath the way she usually did to calm and center herself before walking into the room of a new patient. Only today, instead of an exam room, she walked inside the Appleton Community Church.

She'd awakened early, worried about Abigail West and feeling that nudge. After her morning run, she decided maybe it was time to go back to church—to Jake's church. She hadn't attended regularly since high school. Had thought when she moved to Appleton six months ago that she might visit as a way to meet people. But instead, she'd spent her Sunday mornings either doing rounds at the hospital or relaxing and reading the newspaper, afraid God might not welcome her after she'd pushed Him away for so long.

Well, she hoped God would be okay with her returning. And hoped Jake would show up with Abigail so Violet could check on them.

After the way he got defensive yesterday when she asked about the baby, maybe it was time to suggest he find someone else who could offer advice, someone who could help him with child care. Possibly an older teenager or college student in the church or another parent. Surely someone in this congregation would be willing.

Yes, she was definitely meddling. Still, she wouldn't rest until she knew Jake and Abigail were in good hands.

Violet stepped through the door into the back of the sanctuary. The space was small but beautiful. She stopped and admired the colorful stained glass windows depicting parts of the Bible, stories she'd read as a child each night as her mother or, more often, one of the nannies tucked her in.

Having arrived a bit early, Violet found the crowd was sparse. She'd hoped to run into someone she knew. Instead, she glanced around at strangers, her stomach a tense mass of nerves. She didn't really know anyone well in Appleton, although she had met a few people when she attended the church's fund-raising auction for the Food4Kids program back in the spring.

Violet had bid on and won a trip to a lake house that belonged to two local families. She was acquainted with the daughters of one of the owners. Darcy O'Malley worked in the hospital lab, and they had chatted a few times when Violet dropped by the lab on weekends. She'd later met Darcy's sister, Chloe O'Malley, at her clothing boutique, Chloe's Closet. Maybe one of them would show up for the service.

Violet scanned the sanctuary looking for Grace Hunt, a kind grandmotherly woman who had dropped by to welcome Violet to town when she'd moved in. Grace had invited Violet to the church on several occasions, so surely she would be here today.

At least Violet would know someone besides Jake.

"Hello. Welcome." An elderly man in gray slacks, a navy blazer and a red striped tie approached with his hand extended. "I'm Ted Greer, pastor of the church. You're the new pediatrician, aren't you?"

Shaking his hand, she smiled. "Yes. Violet Crenshaw. I'm sorry it's taken me so long to visit."

His kind eyes warmed. "We're glad you're here now. Do you work on Sundays?"

"I'm usually on call. I should probably apologize ahead of time. I occasionally may have to leave in the middle of the service."

"That's no problem at all. We'd love to have you whenever possible. Maybe next week you can come an hour earlier and join us for Bible study and coffee, as well."

"Oh, okay. I'll consider it." She wasn't sure she was ready for that, though. Needed to meet a few people first.

"If you'll pick up a brochure on the way out, you'll see a listing of Sunday school classes and other small group meetings we have throughout the week. I hope you'll visit around, find a place where you feel comfortable."

"Ted?" someone called from the choir loft while tapping a microphone that appeared to be dead.

"Excuse me for running off," Ted said. "I think they're having trouble with the sound system. Again, welcome. We're glad God brought you here today." He patted her hand, reminding her of her grandfather, and then strode to the front of the church.

Her smile faltered. When she'd left her hometown so many years ago to go to college, severing contact with her parents, she'd hurt her grandfather. Though she'd remained close to him, she'd also disappointed him. On his deathbed, he'd told her he still prayed daily that she would forgive her parents and reconcile. He died having never seen that prayer answered.

And she still hadn't found it in her heart to forgive them for refusing to help her keep her son, for forcing her to give him up for adoption. She hadn't seen her parents since her granddad's funeral, where she'd avoided extended conversation.

Pushing aside the painful memory and the guilt, she steered away from the center aisle and moved to the far left. She inched her way down to about the fourth row from the back and took a seat on the end. As church members entered, they came over to greet her. They were a friendly bunch, making her glad she'd come.

Trying not to be conspicuous, she searched the crowd for Jake in case he'd come in while she was talking. But he wasn't there.

Her shoulders drooped. Had he had a bad night? An infant would certainly make getting ready difficult. Or maybe he didn't attend regularly.

Whatever the reason for his absence, she could still check out possible women in the congregation who could help him with Abigail. As the organist played a prelude, Violet scoped out the room. There were definitely a few young mothers she could try to meet to feel them out, see if they might be available.

Five minutes into the service as the pastor was making announcements, the door behind Violet opened. Maybe it was Jake. Her neck muscles tensed.

She glanced back, and sure enough, Jake was headed down the center aisle wearing khaki pants and a light blue dress shirt with the sleeves rolled up. He carried Abigail's car seat as if it didn't weigh a pound.

Though his beard was neatly trimmed and his hair was freshly washed, the man looked tired. Harried. And he was obviously late.

Had he had trouble giving Abigail a bath? Had

they not gotten any sleep last night? Could there be something wrong with Abigail that Violet had missed?

She snapped her attention back to the front of the church and crossed her arms, her teeth clamped tightly together. Jake was a grown man. She shouldn't worry so much.

Jake slid in the other end of her row—*her row*, of all places. As he set the carrier on the seat beside him, she tried not to stare. Had he spotted her?

She needed to face the front and concentrate on worshipping.

Yet part of the way through the service, when they stood to sing a hymn, she found herself looking over to check on Abigail. Once she realized she couldn't get a clear view of the baby, her gaze wandered upward.

Jake's gaze locked with hers. He didn't crack a smile or spare a wave. The man was used to being the boss at the work site, the one checking up on others. He apparently didn't like thinking someone might be checking up on him.

Well, that was too bad. She wiggled her fingers at him in a friendly wave.

He inclined his head in acknowledgment and then turned back to his hymnbook, singing along until the song came to a close.

Always good at blocking out distractions, Violet sat and tuned in to the pastor's sermon.

When he began to preach about the prodigal son, she stilled.

Seriously?

Had God whispered in Pastor Greer's ear that a wayward believer would show up in need of a good talking-to?

No one in the sanctuary could possibly know how convicted she felt, but Violet's face burned in shame at how she'd tossed aside her faith for more than a decade. Ever since the day fourteen years ago when that little pregnancy test stick had turned positive, when her prayers for help had gone unanswered.

Though Violet wondered if maybe God had been the one to nudge her to come today, she still couldn't bring herself to pray. God probably didn't care to hear from her.

Abigail whimpered. A second whimper cranked up to a good cry, distracting Violet from the message. At the moment, she welcomed the distraction.

Jake looked a bit panicky, rifling through the diaper bag, then popping a pacifier in the baby's mouth.

Apparently, she spit it out because the crying kicked up a notch.

Maybe Violet should scoot over to help.

Jake unhooked the car seat straps and lifted Abigail out, his movements rushed and awkward. Tough to be calm and collected when everyone around was beginning to stare. Even if they were smiling.

He bounced Abigail in his arms, but she wouldn't be consoled.

Violet moved an inch and stopped. Would he think she was interfering?

People turned to look at Jake. He grabbed a bottle and impressed Violet with how quickly he popped it into Abigail's mouth. But she refused it and continued to squall.

With stomach tensing, Violet leaned forward, ready to spring over beside Jake.

Grace Hunt rose from her seat. With her bobbed white hair, she walked up the aisle toward Jake. Smiling, she held out her arms to take the infant. He handed her over along with a pacifier.

As Grace walked away, bouncing Abigail, the crying stopped. Jake heaved a sigh and relaxed against the back of the pew.

Violet had missed her chance. Yet maybe this woman would be the perfect helper for Jake. After the service Violet would suggest Jake ask her for pointers, and maybe Grace could—

Violet's phone vibrated in her pocket. A message from the hospital reporting a five-year-old patient in the ER with dehydration.

On autopilot, she grabbed her purse and slipped into the side aisle, heading toward the exit. Grace stood in the back swaying, holding the pacifier in Abigail's mouth. She smiled and nodded at Violet as she passed. Violet returned the smile, yet couldn't help checking out the baby.

Looking happy and healthy, Abigail sucked on the pacifier while she observed the kind woman holding her.

A wave of disappointment washed over Violet, quickly replaced by irritation. She should not be disappointed that Jake didn't need her help. She should be pleased this woman had offered assistance. Hadn't that been one of Violet's goals for coming today?

Jake had a friend who could teach him to care for the baby. It was time for Violet to return to work mode, to make sure her interest in Jake and Abigail remained strictly professional.

Chapter Three

"You sure are calling early," Aunt Edith said on the other end of the phone line. "It's barely 6:00 a.m."

Jake stood in his kitchen bouncing Abigail in the crook of his arm. She'd been fussy since she woke at five o'clock.

All morning, he'd tried every trick he knew to soothe her, including walking around the yard before dawn and swinging on his childhood swing set while holding Abigail. She would settle for a few minutes but then start fretting again.

Unlike during her nighttime crying jags, at least she was finally taking her bottle this morning.

"What's that noise?" Edith asked. "It sounds like a baby."

"That's because it *is* a baby."

"Is there something you need to tell us?" she said with a laugh.

If only the whole thing were a joke and he could laugh along with her. "Actually, there is. Why don't you put Uncle Paul on the other phone?"

Edith called for her husband to pick up the other extension, telling him Jake had something important to tell them.

"What is it, son?" Paul asked.

"Remy came by a couple of days ago."

Edith gasped. "How is she?"

"She's okay. Looks pretty good, actually. And she's had a baby."

Silence.

"Sorry," Jake said. "Wish I could have prepared you better for that bombshell. But she showed up Friday evening, claiming she's been clean for a year now but saying she's not good mother material. She left the two-week-old baby with me and took off."

"What?" Edith nearly shrieked, probably trying to imagine him taking care of her infant grandchild.

"I don't know what to say." Paul sounded worn-out, as if he'd taken one too many emotional beatings.

Jake's aunt and uncle had been through a great deal of pain and disappointment with their daughter, who'd lied to them, stolen from them and nearly depleted their savings in rehab programs. They'd had to practice tough love for their own sanity.

Once they'd refused to enable her any longer, Remy's rare visits ceased. Because of financial difficulties, the couple had decided to sell their practice and retire early. They moved south to heal.

Jake hated to be the one to reopen the wound. "I'm sorry to call. I tried waiting, hoping she'd come back in a day or two. But she hasn't. I have no contact information. No license plate number. Nothing with an address except hospital records, and who knows if Remy still lives there?"

"We have a grandchild," Edith whispered, tears choking off her voice.

With a whimper, Abigail drew her knees in and spit out the nipple. *Not now.*

"Yes, and Remy put in writing that she wants me to raise her," Jake said.

"We have a granddaughter?"

"Edith," Paul snapped. "A baby isn't going to instantly make us some normal, happy family. She'll come back for the girl, disappear and break our hearts all over again."

His aunt began to cry. Then the phone line clicked as she hung up.

"Uncle Paul?"

"Yeah, I'm still here. What do you plan to do?"

No offer of help. Jake was on his own.

The baby started to fret. He put her to his shoulder and walked outside. What was wrong with her this morning? Was she sick?

"I'll wait it out," Jake said. "I'm sure Remy will come back. In the meantime, I had Dr. Crenshaw check her out."

Paul harrumphed.

"I know we didn't like the terms of the contract, but I think she's a good doctor," Jake said, looking across his backyard to the doc's house.

She sat at the table on her patio. Had she heard him mention her name to his uncle?

"I'm sure she's a good doctor," Paul said. "She had impeccable references. I just didn't like her negotiating. Didn't like her evaluation of our business practices."

Violet stood and started toward him. Great. Just what he needed while his uncle got on a roll.

"Hey, listen. The baby's fussing. I should go."

"You didn't say whether the baby checked out okay."

"She's fine."

"That's a relief. Maybe Remy managed to take decent care of her."

"I need to go. The neighbor's heading this way." He wouldn't specify which neighbor.

"Okay. I imagine Remy will turn up soon, unless, of course, she's back on drugs."

And wasn't that the story of Remy's life? Her problems with drugs had wrecked her life and pretty much destroyed what family Jake had left. "Tell Aunt Edith not to worry about this big clod handling the baby. Doc Crenshaw came over and trained me."

Paul let out a groan. "Don't get sucked in by the pretty doctor. I'm sure Grace Hunt from the church will be glad to help you."

The pretty—more like beautiful—doctor stood in front of him wearing running shorts, an Emory Medical School T-shirt and running shoes. Jake's neck heated. Surely there wasn't any way she'd heard their conversation.

"I'll get the situation figured out," he said to his uncle.

"We can always depend on you, Jake," Paul said. "I'll let you know if by some wild chance we hear from your cousin. Don't tell Edith or it'll get her hopes up, but I'll do some checking to see if I can locate Remy."

"Thanks." They hung up, and he forced a smile for Violet. "Good morning. What's up?"

"I heard Abigail crying earlier when I was out running. Thought I would check on you."

"Making house calls now, huh?" He stuffed the rejected bottle in his pocket, brought Abigail to his shoulder and then gently patted her back. "Come on, sweet thing. Give a nice big burp for Cousin Jake."

Abigail complied by spitting up across his shoulder and down his back.

"What's the deal, Abigail?" he said.

"Some spitting up is normal. Here, let me take her." Violet took the baby and they headed inside the kitchen.

She grabbed a cloth diaper from a freshly washed stack he'd left on the counter. "I'll clean her up."

"Thanks." Jake went to his room to change shirts.

When he returned to the kitchen, Violet was sweet-talking Abigail. She'd changed her into a clean onesie—a new word he'd learned since becoming a temporary guardian. Violet also had the child calmed.

"Thanks. I think my laundry has multiplied tenfold with one tiny little gal."

"Has she acted sick this morning? Is that why you were outside so early?"

"I'm sorry if we disturbed you."

"No, I'm not complaining. Just wondering if everything's okay."

"She woke early and has been fussy. Looks flushed."

Violet placed her lips on Abigail's forehead. "She feels a little warm to me. Did you take her temperature?"

He winced because he had hundreds of dollars of baby paraphernalia but not the equipment he needed. "I apparently missed buying a thermometer."

"I have one. Be right back." She handed over the infant and hurried out the door.

Worried about Abigail and not wanting to drag her to the work site again, he decided he would skip going as planned. There wasn't a lot Jake needed to do that morning anyway, other than check on the cabinet installers and hurry up the interior painters. He texted Zeb. When Zeb didn't reply, he called the man's voice mail to check in and leave instructions.

Violet returned with a bag and pulled out a funny-looking gadget. "Here we go."

"That doesn't look like the thermometers I remember."

She laughed as she gently placed it against Abigail's temple. "You've got to admit this is much more pleasant than the alternative—which, by the way, is my preferred method to measure an accurate temp."

The instrument beeped, and she showed him the result. One hundred degrees. *Now what?*

He glanced at the doctor, searching for signs of concern. "From what I read online this morning it isn't considered a fever until a hundred point four."

"That's a good guideline, but we worry more about the young ones." She brushed back the baby girl's wispy black hair. Felt her neck.

She didn't look too concerned, but his stomach churned anyway. He was not fit to parent a baby. He could set budgets, place orders, coordinate schedules, direct multiple crews of workers and make tough decisions all day long. But throw in a variable like four-tenths of a degree of body temperature and he turned into a bumbling idiot.

Abigail whimpered.

"Why don't we take her temp again?" he said. "Just to make me feel better."

"Sure. I'll show you how."

They went to the living room, and he laid Abigail on the couch. Violet gave him the thermometer and directed him on using it.

Ninety-nine point nine. "Should we be concerned?"

"I doubt it. But I brought my bag, so let me check her over."

His phone vibrated. A new text message.

While she looked in Abigail's ears, he checked the text from Zeb.

Owner said kitchen tile wasn't right color. I checked the order. Is exactly what you told us.

Frustration cinched his gut. Changes cost money and time. I'll look into it. Baby may be sick, he texted back.

"Ears are fine." Violet warmed a stethoscope and listened to Abigail's lungs. "Honestly, she seems fine. Did she cry again last night?"

"From about nine to midnight."

"Looking more like we're dealing with colic."

His phone buzzed again. "Excuse me just a minute. I have a problem at work."

"Go ahead. I'll walk with her outside and see if I can calm her." Violet swaddled the baby in a receiving blanket, then went through the kitchen and out the back door.

The text was from Zeb again. Mrs. E says she hopes you won't let babysitting interfere with your job.

Mrs. Emerson was the owner of one of the homes they were building. She tended to walk around the work site in a business suit and three-inch high heels, breathing down everyone's neck. But Jake wanted her to love her home.

He got Zeb on the phone. "Tell Mrs. Emerson not to worry. I want my customers happy."

"Will do." Zeb snickered. "Baby is fussy, huh? Sounds like you're a regular Mr. Mom."

Jake had seen the man with his grandkids. Zeb had a tough-as-nails exterior and a marshmallow-puff interior. "Yeah, you keep making fun. Next time I see you swinging beside one of your grandkids at the park, you'll never hear the end of it."

"Well, Mr. Mom has a backbone after all."

Jake snorted a laugh. "The girl has been fussy. Temp is a little elevated."

"When in doubt, go to the doctor. Another

excuse to get cozy with the cute new pediatrician who about chewed your rear off Saturday."

Wondering how many people had overheard *that* discussion made his face burn. "The doc is actually here checking her now. But I assure you, there's no coziness where Violet Crenshaw is concerned." A quick glance out the back door gave him a good excuse to avoid the topic. "In fact, I need to go check on them."

"You do that, Jake." Zeb was laughing as he disconnected.

Soft, jet-black hair that smelled like baby shampoo brushed against Violet's cheek, melting her insides. Calm and relaxed, she was pleased her first appointment wasn't until eight-thirty. She didn't need to hurry home.

And Abigail seemed to be relaxing, too. Was getting sleepy.

Jake came out the back door. The sight of him in a T-shirt that molded to his work-toned muscles instantly shot her heart rate up, undoing any soothing from holding Abigail.

"How's she doing?" he asked.

"Better." She smiled at him, knowing he could use some encouragement.

He held up the thermometer he'd brought with him, then took another reading. "Ninety-eight point seven." His shoulders dropped. "That's good. I feel stupid for worrying."

"Don't apologize for erring on the side of caution. Little ones like this can get sick quickly."

"I was afraid I'd done something wrong bathing her last night. Was afraid she'd gotten chilled. She wasn't a happy camper through that nightmare."

Violet bit back a smile. "Bathing will get easier."

"I hope. I think I took too long. She was okay at first, but then the water got cool. She started squalling, all stiff and furious. I bundled her up afterward, making sure she warmed up."

Violet's chest squeezed. The image of this tall, brawny man doing something sweet like warming a chilled baby battered at her heart.

He held out his arms for Abigail.

Hating to give up the warm, sleeping bundle, she handed her over, willing a steel rod into her spine instead of the gelatin this man had put there. "You're doing fine, Jake. Do you think the fussiness this morning seemed different from the crying she's done at night?"

"Definitely. This morning's fussiness hasn't been as severe. At night, no matter what I do to comfort her, she continually shrieks—which, for the record, is horrendous."

"I can imagine."

"I walk the floor, rocking her, singing, cracking dumb jokes, doing everything but standing on my head. It's as if I'm not even there." He shrugged, his eyes troubled. "I've never felt so helpless in my life."

Warning, warning! No melting of heart allowed.

"Today, though, I could console her briefly. She didn't all-out cry, just whimpered and whined."

"Hmm. That does sound more like a baby feeling ill. There's a chance she has a tummy ache or some gas. Are you remembering to burp her after her bottles?"

"Yes. But she has been drawing up her legs as if her stomach hurts. One of my subcontractors mentioned a change of formula curing his grandchild's colic."

Violet would make a note of the stomach pain in Abigail's file. "Every now and then, I've found changing to lactose-free formula does help. How about I bring some samples to you at lunchtime?"

"It would be easier if I just dropped by to pick them up. Besides, I'd feel better if you weighed the little gal. To make sure she's growing okay."

His concern made her stomach swoop. "I'll be happy to weigh her for you. Come by at noon."

"Great, thanks."

Jake carefully wrapped the blanket tighter around Abigail, every tuck of the fabric jarring loose more of the protective barrier from around

Violet's heart, releasing the longing she'd held at bay for so long.

Longing for a husband of her own and a baby to love.

She worked with babies every day. Why was Abigail different?

Could the difference be Jake? What was it about him that gave her crazy notions of love and family?

He rubbed his big, strong hand over Abigail's tiny head. It hit her then why Jake affected her so. It was because he was a single guy suddenly stuck with a baby.

A guy who needed Violet's help.

Cold rushed through her veins. She absolutely could not allow herself to fall into the being-needed trap. That's how she'd gotten sucked into an inappropriately intense—and intimate—relationship with Hank in high school. And ended up pregnant.

She would never, ever again get sucked in by a needy man.

Jake's not really needy, a little niggling voice said. *He's not manipulating you, demanding your total devotion. He's just a strong man in a temporary, unfamiliar situation.*

He kissed the baby's forehead and then looked into Violet's eyes. The moment went on longer than normal—too long—and suddenly something flared between them.

Violet could barely breathe. "We're usually closed at lunch, so if no one is at the front desk, come on back to the first exam room."

"Okay. We'll see you at noon." His grateful smile did crazy things to her insides.

"I, uh, need to get to the office." She shot toward the row of hedges between their houses, escaping the handsome babysitter who made her want things she feared wanting.

A grinning puppy with human-like teeth mocked Jake.

The pup was pictured on a giant, kid-friendly poster hanging on the wall in the pediatric exam room. This whole scenario—him in the former office of the family who raised him, being questioned about a baby who shouldn't be in his care by the woman who had "bought" the practice from them—was laughable. Sad, but laughable.

Violet, who'd been so helpful that morning, had turned back into serious doctor mode at the office. "Here are the samples." She pointed to a bag. "Abigail's weight is good. She's gained a couple of ounces, which is right on target. Before we try changing her formula, I'd like to first consult with her mother or her regular pediatrician."

"I have written permission from Remy to make decisions for Abigail."

"Still, I'd like to find out what they've fed her in the past. Find out if she had any complications at birth." She gave a tense smile and waited, refusing to retreat.

He felt as if the signed document was useless. The phone number Remy had listed on it was a dead end. Disconnected.

"I want to go ahead and try the samples," he said.

"If you know the name of the regular pediatrician, I can give the office a quick call."

"I'm afraid I don't."

"Can you call Remy to ask?" On the rolling stool that had once been his uncle's perch, the doctor sat with a stethoscope around her neck, a pen in her hand and a disgruntled look on her face.

No wonder. None of the situation made a lick of sense if she didn't know the whole story.

He couldn't cover for Remy forever. But what if Violet chose to call in the authorities? Jake did not want Abigail put in the system. It had happened to him after his parents died, before his aunt and uncle agreed to take him.

Jake looked down at Abigail, who was once again nodding off, content for the moment. The quiet times, times when she looked so peaceful in his arms, settled inside him like a warm blanket.

Three nights with her, and already he was attached.

He looked up at Violet. "I haven't been able to get hold of Remy."

"What do you mean?"

The thought of Remy never showing up made his lungs squeeze. How would he manage?

"Jake? How long will your cousin be gone?"

"I don't know when she'll return. Maybe never."

Violet sucked in a breath through her nose, but the expression on her face remained neutral. A real professional. "Is this a new development?"

He nailed her with his gaze, praying she'd understand. "I thought she would come back by now. I'm going to have to find her."

"Remy gave you this medical consent," she said, waving the file folder, "but then decided not to return?"

What if he never found her? What if he found her, but she refused to take Abigail back? His heart slammed against his chest as he debated telling Violet the last piece of the story.

The doctor sat waiting.

"When Remy dropped off the baby, she said she wants me to raise her daughter." He pulled the handwritten and signed piece of lined notebook paper out of the diaper bag and handed it to her.

Violet's professional aloofness cracked. Concern put a wrinkle in her forehead, which didn't do a thing to boost his confidence. "That's not official."

"Maybe not. But it's all I know at the moment."

"Why would she want to give up her child?"

Abigail let out a little whimper and stiffened her legs. He rubbed her tummy.

"My cousin has had some drug problems in the past." Problems he'd tried like crazy to fix but had never been able. "Though she said she's been clean for over a year, I don't know what kind of situation she's in."

"What about the father?"

"He died and has no family."

Nodding, Violet rolled her stool closer and smoothed the baby's hair, almost as if she needed to comfort her for having a disappearing mom. The doc could be a kind, compassionate woman—when she wanted to be.

"I'm sorry," she said. "For Abigail, and for you, Edith and Paul."

"Thanks."

Her hazel eyes met his, and the warm, tender look he'd seen was gone. "But the authorities should be involved."

His insides froze. "I'm not letting Abigail go into the foster care system, not when Remy wants her with me. I'll find Remy and we'll work it out."

"Do you really believe she's gotten clean?"

"She seemed different the other day. Almost as if she was truly sad to leave the baby but was doing what she thought best for her daughter." Although she'd been hard as well, hard and still bitter toward him.

Violet chewed the inside of her lip as if unsure, as if weighing her options.

How would he possibly deal with handling a baby long-term? Pushing down the panic, he focused on keeping Abigail out of foster care. "My uncle is also trying to track Remy down. We need some time."

Her gaze clashed with his. "I'm just thinking of the welfare of the child."

"I can respect that. I promise you, if we don't find Remy soon, I'll contact a lawyer to figure out the next step."

"What if you find her, and she's back on drugs?"

Jake had no idea what he'd do. Had no idea what Edith and Paul would want to do.

But he couldn't go there right now. "At this point, I have to assume the best outcome—that Remy is clean and will want to raise her child."

Pain flashed in Violet's eyes. "Sometimes circumstances make that impossible."

"I guess we'll find out. In the meantime, I'm going to make sure Abigail stays with family." Jake slipped the girl back in her car seat and buckled the straps. Then he put the new formula in the diaper bag. "Thanks for the samples."

Violet observed him through squinted eyes as if trying to see inside him, to test his character. "Call if she's not better in a couple of days."

"I will." A tense breath eased out of him.

Would she let him deal with their family situation as he saw fit?

She drummed her fingers on the exam table, crinkling the paper covering, as she stared at the baby. "Abigail is well cared for, so I won't make any calls right now. I'll give you, Edith and Paul time. But I'll be checking on her."

Sawing his teeth back and forth, he bit back the retort that nearly flew out of his mouth. "I may not know a lot about infants, but Abigail is my flesh and blood. You can rest assured I'll protect her."

A knock sounded on the door, and the nurse, someone Jake didn't know, stuck her head inside. "Dr. Crenshaw, we're back from lunch, and your first patient is waiting for you."

The young woman didn't look pleased that the man and baby who'd barged in during lunch were still there.

"Remember," Violet said to Jake. "Keep in touch." She snapped the medical file closed and zipped out of the room.

Jake had to get out of there and find Remy. And he had to do it before Violet changed her mind about calling the authorities.

Chapter Four

Birds busily chirped and whistled as Violet finished her morning run. She bent over, resting her hands on her thighs and sucking in air, then forced herself up to walk two laps around the perimeter of the yard to cool down. When she reached the patio, she stretched her tired muscles. *How many patients will I see today?* She still needed to check the calendar and hoped this week would bring in more income than last week.

How much will the July electric bill be? It's been so hot this summer.

The sunrise lightened the sky from gray to a pale blue as she pulled in a slow, deep breath, held it, then released it, expelling worries that tried to intrude. She refused to brood over how Jake's grumbling around town had affected her ability to bring in patients.

Did Abigail have a good night?

No. Don't go there. She needed to use the early-morning time wisely.

Violet never needed an alarm clock. Hadn't since her teens. Something internal woke her every morning between four and five o'clock, and then her thoughts—of the past and of the present—kept her awake. In the beginning, the early rising frustrated her. But since moving into this house, she'd learned to battle the frustration by being productive. She'd usually run to burn off tension, then spend time outside preparing for the day by studying patient cases or reviewing her schedule.

If nothing else, she was a pro at taking old wounds and regrets and pushing them away.

She grabbed her water bottle and guzzled. Then she went inside, kicked off her shoes and socks and slipped into her favorite worn flip-flops. The aroma of coffee drew her to the pot that had brewed on a timer while she was out.

Drawing comfort from the rituals, Violet found routine helped control thoughts that invariably tried to intrude. She couldn't allow a moment of worry over her relationship with her parents, or what her son might look like, or when her practice would make a profit. She needed to work hard and push ahead.

With a cup of steaming coffee laced with hazelnut creamer, she went outside to sit on the patio. Touching the screen of her tablet, she pulled up her schedule for the day. The first patient was a four-year-old who'd had a persistent cough. She'd tried two rounds of the same antibiotic, so maybe she'd try a different class. She also needed to consider cough-variant asthma. And order a chest X-ray to make sure she wasn't missing something.

The sound of human voices joined in with the chorus of birds.

Or rather, the sound of one human. A male voice pitched into a high register.

She turned from her place at the table and spotted Jake in his backyard holding Abigail, cooing to her.

The silly tone made her smile. And put a dent in her concentration. She might as well go check on Abigail, one thing she could mark off her to-do list for the day.

As she walked across the dewy yard carrying her coffee mug, flip-flops snapping against her heels, she ran fingers through her hair. Hesitant, she slowed. She wore no makeup. Her hair was damp with perspiration. And her running clothes—shorts and a faded T-shirt—weren't exactly ideal for visiting neighbors. Especially a handsome, single neighbor.

With a huff, she tromped ahead. This wasn't a neighborly visit. And it certainly didn't matter that her neighbor was handsome or single. This was strictly a professional check on a patient.

Yeah, and you're looking real professional right now, Violet.

Jake sat squeezed into a swing attached to an old rusty swing set that had probably been his and Remy's when they were growing up. With Abigail in his lap, her head on his knees and her feet pressed into his belly, he leaned his face closer to her. "Come on, give ol' Jake a smile," he said in the silly singsong voice.

"I'm afraid she won't give you a social smile until she's around six to eight weeks old."

His head jerked up. "Oh. Good morning. You're out early again, I see."

"I'm always out at sunrise year-round. Watching the sun come up, preparing for my day."

"By design or insomnia?"

"By my internal clock, I guess. I haven't used an alarm clock since I was about eighteen."

"Abigail is now my alarm and seems to favor waking at about five, an hour before my norm."

She was pleased he didn't act frustrated. Seemed to take what Abigail threw at him. "Was she fussing like yesterday?"

"No. Just bright-eyed and ready to eat. Which, by the way, is going better so far. No more drawing up her legs."

"That's good news."

"Care to join us?" he asked, nodding toward the other swing.

"You think the old set can hold both of us?"

With a laugh, he quickly looked her over from head to toe, measuring her size. "I guess we'll find out."

As she gently slid into the swing, she checked out the baby. "Abigail looks good this morning. Like you said, very alert and bright-eyed."

"Yeah. She cried some last night, but not as long. I feel half human today."

He definitely didn't look any worse for the wear. "You'll be amazed at how good you'll feel once she sleeps through the night. Of course, many parents panic when they wake and realize it's morning."

"I can imagine."

Would Remy return before that point? If so, would Abigail be safe with her mother? "How is the Remy search going?"

"Since the phone number on hospital records is disconnected, I'm going to check into the address this morning." Jake tucked the blanket around the baby and lifted her to the crook of his arm. "I plan to call Grace Hunt, who rescued me during the service last Sunday, and ask if she'll help with child care."

"Sounds like a great idea. Abigail settled nicely with her."

"Yeah, a huge relief after we caused a ruckus."

Violet bit back a grin and could relate to not wanting to make a scene—ever. "What if Grace can't babysit?"

"I'll ask her for recommendations."

"I saw several potential babysitters on Sunday. And maybe I could help in a pinch," Violet said before fully considering the offer. What was she thinking?

"Wouldn't that mess with your work schedule?"

With a push of her foot, she set the swing in motion, embarrassed. Sure, she needed to keep tabs on Abigail. But babysitting? "Well, my afternoons tend to be slow until after parents get off from work."

"What about tomorrow?" he asked, a hopeful smile lifting his brows. "I really need to get to a couple of work sites. Without a baby."

She sighed, wishing she hadn't already looked at the week's schedule. "Tomorrow afternoon is open so far."

"I'm working from home today, putting together an estimate and calling suppliers. But I'd love to let the crew know I'll be there tomorrow."

"I'll pencil that in. But please ask Grace first."

"Will do. It's nice to have a backup plan, though." He smiled, and the look of gratitude did funny things to her insides. Made her glad she could put that look on his face.

She popped off the swing, almost as dramatic as the midair dismounts she'd done as a kid. *What a dork.* Thankfully her mug was empty or she would have splashed the creamy mess all over herself. "Well, gotta go get ready for work."

"Thanks," he called to her back as she hurried toward home.

She'd already veered off her morning routine. Would feel behind and rushed for the rest of the day, thanks to a man and a baby.

A really sweet baby she might be babysitting tomorrow.

What had she potentially gotten herself into?

"Are you serious?"

"I am," Jake said to Zeb over the phone. Because Zeb was there putting in flooring, Jake had asked him to cover for him—something Jake had never done. Had never even considered. Naturally, Zeb would be surprised.

"Until I can arrange for child care, I can't be there as much as I'd like," Jake said. "I'll be by when I can."

"You know I'm happy to help, but what's going on?"

Jake heaved a sigh. "I wasn't totally up front with you when I said I'm babysitting Remy's baby. She actually took off and left Abigail here with me."

"Ah, man. That's tough."

"I plan to locate Remy and talk her into coming home."

"I've got you covered. Do what you need to do."

"Thanks, Zeb. I owe you."

When they hung up, Jake peeked in on a peacefully napping Abigail. He grabbed the baby monitor and sat at the kitchen table to open his laptop.

With Remy's papers beside him, he compared her address on the documents. All the same. An Atlanta address. He typed it in a search engine.

Several entries came up. The top of the search was something called Peace House. He clicked a link to take him to the site.

A domestic violence shelter? His heart thudded as he sucked in a breath. "Oh, no." Surely not.

Quickly searching the site, he discovered the address did match Remy's paperwork. The phone number matched, too.

The website said the number was for administrative offices. But previous calls had turned up a recording saying the number was no longer in service.

Could Remy have made up the address? Or chosen it to throw him off track? He could only hope so. Maybe she wanted to keep her real address private.

But why? Unless she was hiding.

A sick feeling of dread settled in his stomach. Could she have lied about Abigail's father being dead? Was she trying to keep Abigail from an abusive father?

Lord, I pray Remy is okay. Please protect her, and help her stay clean.

Jake searched the shelter's website further and found the director's name and email contact. He quickly sent a message to Florence Phillips.

His need to find Remy, to know the truth, had just doubled in urgency.

He had to know how to protect Abigail.

Until he heard back from the shelter email, the only thing he could do was to go in person to check it out for himself. Which meant he needed a babysitter for more than the couple of hours Violet could spare.

He picked up the phone to call Grace Hunt's number and got an immediate answer.

"Miss Grace, this is Jake West."

"Oh, hello, Jake. How's that adorable baby doing?"

"She's doing better every day. In fact, that's why I'm calling. I was wondering if I could hire you to babysit for me."

The kind, elderly woman let out a sigh. "I wish I could, dear. But I have a jam-packed schedule right now. How long are you keeping the baby for Remy?"

Now that he'd told Violet and Zeb about Remy's disappearing act, Grace would soon hear. News traveled quickly in their small town.

"Grace, I don't know when or if she'll be back." He went on to explain the whole situation and about how Violet had shown him how to care for Abigail.

"Oh, you poor man. I'm sure you need a lot of help, what with your business to run and all." She let out a huff. "I suggest you ask that pretty pediatrician to watch the baby whenever she can. Could be God brought you two together for a reason."

Jake's neck radiated heat like a 100,000 BTU gas furnace. "I appreciate your advice." But if he had to ask Violet for help, it wouldn't be because she was pretty or that God had brought them together for a reason.

In fact, he needed to be cautious. The woman might try to insert herself in his family matter. He had to keep her on his side.

"In the meantime, Grace, can you suggest any young women in the church I could possibly hire?"

"Well, that little Kelli Calhoun is in college now, taking summer classes. And the Brockett girl, bless her heart, works down at the IGA every weekday at 7:00 a.m., sometimes staying as late as 7:00 p.m. Hmm…let me see…" She paused for breath. "The Stephens twins are already babysitting full-time. That cute redheaded Emily is on the swim team, but maybe she'd have a bit of time?"

"She's only in middle school. What about some young moms?"

"Just between you and me, Liza could probably use the extra money. But, Jake, honey, she already has four small children, and I don't see how she could possibly care for another child as young as your Abigail."

His shoulders felt as if they weighed a hundred pounds. "And you can't think of anyone else?"

"Not a single one right now. But I'll let you know if I do."

Jake thanked her and hung up. If Grace and everyone else she knew were unavailable, it looked as if he was going to need Violet more than he'd anticipated. If he called on her too often or let her get too close, though, would she decide he wasn't capable of caring for Abigail and try to intervene?

Violet approached the homey bungalow with some trepidation on Wednesday just after noon. Could she really babysit Abigail while remaining a neutral bystander, offering assistance as needed without attachment?

The front door opened, and Jake appeared wearing work-worn jeans and a company-logo T-shirt. His hair stood up as if he'd been jamming his hand through it. And he certainly didn't look welcoming.

Maybe it wasn't too late to back out. "Do you still need me to babysit?"

"I do. I've got a situation and need to get to the work site pronto."

Assistance without attachment. "Where's Abigail?"

He motioned her inside ahead of him. As she brushed past him and filled her nose with his clean, woodsy scent, she had to admit that he was easy on the nose...and the eyes.

Every time she entered his house, she felt at home. Comfortable.

Maybe comfortable was okay. But she shouldn't allow herself to feel so drawn to him or to the baby. Not when the baby was most likely temporary.

Jake's not temporary, though.

Jake leaned down in front of her face and smiled.

She'd missed what he'd said. "Excuse me?"

"I was saying the little gal just woke from a nap. I changed her diaper and put her in the bouncy seat."

On the floor beside the couch, Abigail kicked her feet, making the seat jiggle.

"You've bought her more paraphernalia?" Violet asked.

His neck reddened at her question. "Yeah. I figured she was getting sick of looking at my chest."

Violet's eyes darted to his broad chest and doubted anyone would tire of that scenery.

She dragged her gaze away and nodded toward the baby seat with brightly colored toys suspended above it. "Yes, visual stimulation is nice."

"Thanks again for coming. In case you need me…" He offered his cell phone. "Can we switch numbers?"

"Oh, sure." She handed over hers and added her phone number to his contacts. Then they switched back.

It felt like such a date-type thing to do, so personal, that it made her heart flutter in her chest.

"Listen," he said. "I have another favor to ask already."

"Sure."

"Don't say that so quickly. This is a biggie." He ran a hand through his unruly brown hair. "I checked out Remy's address from the hospital records. It's a place called Peace House in Atlanta. From their website, it appears to be a domestic violence shelter."

Violet gasped. "Jake, no."

"Yeah, that was my reaction." He winced, his eyes sad. "The phone is disconnected. I emailed them through the website but got no answer. I'd like to go to the address, in Atlanta, to investigate."

"I think that's a good idea."

"I wanted to impose again and ask if you can

either babysit Abigail or…" He looked into her eyes. "Or go with me to help with the baby."

"What if the father's still alive and Remy has been trying to protect Abigail?"

"That occurred to me, too," he said.

The thought of Abigail being in danger from an abusive father made Violet's stomach drop.

If Jake somehow found Remy, would he turn the baby over to her mother? Violet wanted to be there to assess the situation. "Most domestic violence shelters are in undisclosed locations. But I think you do need to check the address she left you. I'd like to go with you…in case… well, in case Abigail needs me." Her face burned because she wasn't just worried about the baby.

"What day's good for you?"

She lifted her chin and put on her business face. "How about I try to clear my schedule for Friday?"

He let out a deep breath as if he'd been holding it. Yet the crease between his brows didn't ease. "All right. I'll arrange it."

Staring into each other's eyes, neither seemed to know what to say.

Days ago, she would have thought of him as her worst enemy. And he probably felt the same.

Strange how concern for a tiny baby could bring two people together.

Jake suddenly jerked his gaze away and clapped his hands together. "Well, I've got to go. Diapers are by the changing table in the first bedroom on the left. And there are more in the diaper bag."

"That's fine. Would you mind if I take Abigail to the grocery store? I figured I could take care of some of my errands."

"Don't mind at all if it'll help you. I just hope she'll cooperate."

The baby gave a little peep of irritation as if ready to fuss.

"I guess that's my cue to leave," Jake said with a laugh. "There's an extra house key in the diaper bag. I'll put her car seat base in your car on the way out."

As soon as Jake left, the infant let out an irritated cry. Violet picked her up, and she settled immediately with the contact.

She packed up the diaper bag and then put Abigail in the carrier. Once she had the safety seat clicked in place, they drove to the store.

It felt like such a normal motherly thing to do—parking and carrying the baby carrier inside.

Violet attached the seat to the grocery cart. Pulling out her short shopping list, she headed to the produce aisle.

She stopped to look at bell peppers. "Hmm, what do you think, sweet girl? Should I buy red or yellow?"

Abigail gazed at her with big blue eyes and

blew little spit bubbles. As Violet kissed a tiny hand, her heart swelled.

Another customer reached for a green pepper. "What a precious baby. And she's being so good!"

"Yes, she's a sweet one."

Abigail's tiny hand tightened around Violet's finger, and invisible fingers seemed to wrap around her heart as well, plucking at the damaged heartstrings, heartstrings ripped apart when her child had been taken away.

With a brush of Abigail's soft hair, Violet tried to rebuild the fortress that shielded her from longing for things of the past. But, for just a moment, Violet had glimpsed what it would have been like to raise a child she'd brought into the world, if circumstances had been different, if her parents had worried less about what the community thought and more about what was best for their daughter and grandchild.

"Hi, Violet."

She glanced behind her and found Chloe O'Malley, who must've taken a break from her clothing boutique to do some shopping.

"Oh, hi, Chloe."

"Whose baby?"

"Jake West's...well, his cousin's baby."

"So Remy had a baby?"

"Yes, this is Abigail. And she's staying with Jake for a while."

Chloe's eyes widened. "Wow. I bet that's entertaining."

Violet couldn't stop the laugh that burst out. "He was pretty clueless at first. But with a little tutoring, he's doing a good job."

"Tutoring…by you?" Chloe's silvery-blue eyes sparkled with curiosity.

"Yes. He brought her to me at the office to examine."

"I seeee." Her tone—filled with innuendo— made Violet's face heat.

Maybe the woman did see a little too much. "Don't look at me like that. It's not what you think."

"Isn't it? I think I see potential in this situation. Dating potential."

The laughter in Chloe's eyes wrung an unwilling smile from Violet. She shook her head and bit her lip.

The fact that she was at the grocery store with Jake's charge during the middle of a workday probably did suggest more than just a favor. "Don't look so thrilled about it. Jake's just stuck without a babysitter, and I offered to fill in for a couple of hours this afternoon."

"Uh-huh." She grinned. "Nice job catching the most eligible bachelor in town. You need to use the lake house trip you won at the Food-4Kids auction and invite him along. Pick a date and we'll arrange it."

Before Violet could further correct the misperception, Chloe darted off.

Violet wanted to growl, to chase Chloe down and tell her to drop the silly notion that there was anything more going on than babysitting.

But she had no recourse. And still had groceries to buy. So she pushed aside the teasing and marched ahead, checking each item off the list.

Abigail cooperated beautifully until Violet was in the last aisle picking up milk. The good little shopper started to kick her feet and fuss.

"I know. You've been such a good girl. Just give me one more minute." She zipped the cart toward the checkout line.

She groaned when she found customers backed up two or three deep at every register. Who knew Wednesday afternoon could be so crowded? Was it double coupon day?

Violet lifted Abigail out of the seat and held her as they waited. When she finally reached the cash register, she managed to pay with her one free hand and then asked for help out with her purchases.

A teenaged boy pushed the cart to her car. As he grabbed two of the plastic bags, she reached in the cart to help.

"Here, let me do that," said Jake from behind her, sending her heart racing and chill-bumps rising along the little hairs at the back of her neck.

"Oh. Thanks."

How could the deep voice of the man cause such a strong reaction? Could be the close proximity. Or the heat of his arm as he took the bag out of her hand and placed it in the trunk.

Jake thanked the boy and sent him back inside. Then he reached around her to finish transferring the groceries to the car.

She stepped aside to give him room, trying to gather her wits. She was not some giggly, naive girl with a crush on a guy. She was a grown woman running a business. She'd been on her own and supported herself for years.

Sure, it was nice to have a man show up and offer to do something helpful. But that was no reason for her stupid, irritating reaction.

He loaded the last bag with the eggs and then slammed the trunk closed. When he straightened, he looked into her eyes, a gentle smile on his face.

She slowly drew in a deep breath.

He reached toward her and…brushed a finger across Abigail's cheek. "Hey there, sweet thing."

"I didn't expect to see you here," Violet said, trying not to sound as rattled as she felt by his nearness.

"Yeah." He looked adoringly at his baby cousin. "I did what I most needed to do at work. But then I wanted to get back to my girl and remembered you saying you needed to go to the grocery store."

Violet felt as if the walls of her chest were crushing her lungs. Tears stung her nose as she watched how tenderly he treated Abigail. At how devoted he was to her already.

"She was a real trouper," she said through a tight throat. "Didn't make a peep until time to go through checkout."

He reached for the baby. "I'm glad."

He smelled the same as earlier but enhanced with the faint aroma of sawdust and sunshine. She wanted to lean in, plaster herself against him to take in more of the appealing scent. To lean into strong arms that could be both gentle and devoted.

No. She couldn't allow that type of fantasy to take hold. She quickly put space between them.

"We can go ahead and transfer Abigail's stuff," he said. "That way you can go straight home to put your food away."

Her shoulders drooped, but she ratcheted them up. "Oh, okay. I'll do that since your hands are full."

Once she put the car seat and diaper bag in his truck, she brushed a hand across Abigail's soft head. "Be good for Jake, sweetie."

Time for the pretend motherhood to end. Unfortunately, she'd toyed with the idea too much that day. Had enjoyed the shopping trip with

Abigail too much. Had enjoyed meeting up with Jake too much, as well.

Across the parking lot, a waving hand drew Violet's attention. It was Chloe O'Malley again. When Violet returned the wave, Chloe gave a thumbs-up.

Too bad reality would disappoint her new friend.

Fearing Jake would read the disappointment on her face, she drew back her shoulders and looked directly into his gorgeous blue eyes. "Expect me around ten o'clock on Friday. I may need to see a few sick patients early that morning, but I should be free by ten."

"That's perfect. Thanks for today."

The man wore grateful well. And he wore the hunky dad look well, too.

Why had no one snatched him up yet?

She quickly escaped inside her car—she who'd always faced life head-on. And now, in the space of a week, she'd run from this man— or rather, her attraction to him—two or three times.

Could she help him without getting sucked in? Because there suddenly seemed to be a very fine line between assistance and attachment.

Chapter Five

With the help of the map app on his cell phone and Violet's knowledge of the area, Jake steered his truck through downtown Atlanta traffic.

Abigail slept peacefully in the backseat as Violet sat quietly beside him. She wore perfectly pressed khaki slacks and a summery silk blouse in a soft yellow color that made her look feminine. It reminded him of one of Aunt Edith's expressions—a breath of fresh air.

"Let's get off at the next exit," Violet said. "We'll miss some traffic on The Connector."

Following her directions, he drove down the exit ramp. High-rise office buildings swallowed them as they wove their way along smaller roads, deeper into the city.

"I appreciate you showing me the back way," he said. "We seem to have avoided some of the worst bottlenecks and one-way streets."

"When I was a resident, I moonlighted at a

couple of Atlanta hospitals." Brushing back the flippy edges of her hair, she smiled. "I learned all the shortcuts."

"Must've been tough working all those hours." He glanced over at her. "I imagine you were a serious student."

Chuckling, she shook her head. "Yeah, you can say that. Definitely determined."

"I'm sure your parents are proud."

When she didn't immediately answer, he looked over.

"Oh, slow down," she said, pointing at the next street sign. "We need to turn there."

She still didn't acknowledge his comment. Could she be avoiding the topic of her parents? Interesting.

Jake took a right and then went left one block later. At their destination, he parked in a small pay lot. The area had a few boarded-up buildings but otherwise looked like a small community. Across the street he spotted a pawnshop and dry cleaners. On their side of the street were a tiny grocery store, a barbershop and a deli. Power poles were papered with layer upon layer of faded concert and event posters.

"I don't think we're going to find a shelter for women and children around here," Violet said as she climbed out of the truck.

Jake opened the back door and removed Abigail's carrier seat. "Doesn't look residential at all, does it?"

They walked along the sidewalk.

"Oh, look. Here's a building number." Violet indicated a peeling painted address over the doorway of the deli. "Nine sixty-two."

"Then we need to look on the other side of the street." He touched her elbow as they waited for two cars to pass before crossing. Full of energy, she searched for their address a step ahead of him, her flowery scent drifting his way.

"There it is."

Sure enough, the place had a worn sign on the door stating they'd found Peace House. The interior looked dark. He pulled the door handle, but it was locked.

Frustrated, he groaned. "What a waste."

"No, it was worth the trip." She held her hands to the glass to look inside. "There's still furniture here. Maybe it's not closed permanently."

"With the phone disconnected?" Shaking his head, he let out a sigh. "I can't believe Remy was in danger, escaped somewhere like this and didn't tell anyone in our family."

The idea of her being mistreated by a man who was supposed to love her made him want to punch a fist through the glass.

With her eyes still between cupped hands, Violet moved from window to window, surveying the interior. "I don't think she ever stayed here. It's only a small office."

"Regardless, it's a dead end."

"Don't give up so quickly." She stepped off the curb and glanced up and down the street. "Come on. Let's go do some investigative work."

A vise lifted from his chest, and he found himself breathing deeper. It was nice to have someone on his side. He hefted Abigail's carrier a little higher. "Lead on."

Like a hound with its nose in the air, Violet eyed each of the surrounding shops, checking out the signs, peeking inside. The thought of her possibly stopping someone walking down the street to ask questions made him smile.

He was seeing a new side of Violet Crenshaw. Probably the determined side she mentioned earlier.

"Come on," she said. "I think this is a good place to start."

They waited for an elderly couple to pass, then opened the door and entered the mini-market. The inside was dimly lit and somewhat grungy. A lone employee was leaned over, restocking a shelf with potato chips.

"Excuse me," Violet said, her sweet voice like sunshine in the dim recesses of the crowded aisles.

The man continued to slap small bags of chips into a display rack. "What?" he grumbled.

"Do you know if Peace House is still in business?" she asked.

"Ain't got no clue."

"Have women been living there?"

He smashed a fist through the packing tape of an empty box and flattened it, then zipped open another package with a box cutter. "No clue."

"So you haven't seen staff or guests coming or going lately?"

Bent over the box, not bothering to look Violet in the eye, he sighed as if extremely put out. "Does it look like we've got a Hilton around here?"

Jake clenched his fist, fighting the urge to knock the man six blocks over to that particular hotel. "Hey, man. You don't have to be rude."

"And if you're not a paying customer, I'd say it's time to move along."

Jake pulled Abigail protectively closer as he nodded Violet toward the door. "Come on."

They stepped out into the sunlight, and Abigail cringed at the brightness. He pulled open the built-in fabric canopy on her carrier to shade her face.

"Well, so much for my keen eye," Violet said.

He couldn't help but grin. "Who could've guessed Mr. Personality would work there?"

A laugh burst out of her. "I wish you could have seen your jaw twitching where you must've been grinding your teeth."

"Believe me, I was sorely tempted to say something that's not very nice. He didn't have to be so sarcastic with you."

"Well, I appreciate you standing up for me."

Her smile was so lovely, he wanted to reach out and trace it with his fingers.

She pulled her gaze away, glanced at the ground, then looked back up to the storefronts. "Let's go in the pawnshop."

The folks there ended up being nice but had no idea what was going on at Peace House. Next they tried the dry cleaners.

When they exited, Violet wore a perky expression. "Well, that helped some."

"You're such an optimist," Jake said with a chuckle. "The pawnshop clerk said she'd seen a worker at Peace House last week. I don't know how you find that helpful."

She shrugged. "It's better than a poke in the eye."

"Or a man grunting 'No clue'?"

"Yeah. See? We should be thankful for every scrap of info."

He shook his head, yet he couldn't help the smile that spread across his face and wouldn't go away as he followed her across the street.

"Hey, look. There's a beauty shop," she said. "That could be a gold mine."

As they approached, Abigail started to cry.

"She's got to be hungry," he said.

"Here, I'll feed her while you talk to the ladies inside."

Holding Abigail in the crook of her left arm, Violet popped a bottle in the baby's mouth. Abigail greedily slurped it down.

Jake held the door for Violet, and they stepped inside. The smell of chemicals nearly bowled him over and made his nose crinkle.

Violet stifled a laugh. "Not your usual hangout, huh?"

"Hardly."

Two stylists stood at stations with customers. One snipped at the ends of a young woman's long dark hair. The stylist looked like something out of the fifties, wearing a poufy hairstyle and an old-fashioned waitress outfit.

The other stylist squirted something liquid on the white hair of an older woman, hair that was wrapped around colorful curler things. He suspected the solution was the source of the chemical smell.

"Hi, folks. How can I help you?" asked the one in the pink waitress uniform.

Jake nodded at them. "Good morning, ladies. Do y'all know if Peace House is still in business?"

The hands of the hairdresser stilled. Her eyes narrowed. "Why are you asking?"

"I believe my cousin lives there. I'm trying to locate her."

The young woman in the seat, whose back was to him, glared at him in the mirror.

He could understand their concerns.

Violet stepped closer with a pleasant, friendly expression. "We read online that it's a shelter for victims of domestic violence. I assure you, Jake here is not a husband or boyfriend of a resident. He just wants to help his cousin."

Fifties Woman seemed to relax a bit. "The shelter itself is in a secret location. The office is only open a couple of days a week. But they won't give you any information. You'll have to email the address on the website. If your cousin is a resident, they'll pass along your message to her."

"And if she's no longer there?" he asked.

"I doubt they'll give any forwarding information."

Secret location. Limited access. But they were dealing with an organization designed to protect. He'd have to be patient and let the system work. A system that might be protecting his own family.

Anxiety clenched at his gut. Was Remy safe? "Thanks for your help. I've already emailed them. I guess I'll have to wait and pray I find Remy."

Something flared in the stylist's eyes. Did she know Remy? He pulled out a business card and handed it to her. "I'd appreciate it if you'd call me if you run into my cousin. I want to help her."

The woman glanced at Abigail as she reached out with long, hot-pink fingernails and took the card. "Will do." She read Jake's information, then tucked it in a pocket of her little white apron.

"Thanks for your help," Violet said.

"Yeah, we appreciate it." Jake hoisted the diaper bag and then picked up the carrier.

Lifting a section of hair, the stylist gave two brisk snips. "The three of you make a beautiful family."

His heart gave a jolt. He wasn't going to go into details of his situation with strangers. It could put Abigail at risk. "Uh, thanks." His gaze snapped to Violet, who glanced away, her cheeks flushed.

Fifties Woman and the other stylist shared a look.

They knew something.

"Well, I'll give you a call if I find out anything about your cousin. Remy…?"

"Remy West." He nodded as he held the door for Violet. "Thanks again." Following her out, he grabbed the salon's business card off the checkout counter.

Dotty's Dippity-Do
Dotty Simmons, Owner

As soon as the door closed behind them,

Violet spun around to face him. "They know something."

"I agree. We have to hope they'll decide I'm safe and will contact me. Or they'll at least contact Remy if they know where she is."

"Yeah. I'm afraid that's as close as we're going to get for now."

Abigail pushed out the bottle. Violet burped her and then placed her in the carrier.

"Hey," he said. "Sorry about the lie of omission in there. About us being a family..."

"Oh, no big deal." As she leaned over the baby and adjusted the seat straps the back of her neck flushed.

For some odd reason, he wanted to smooth a hand over the blush, cooling the heat. Instead, he pushed the diaper bag farther up his shoulder, then ushered Violet toward the car.

Today might feel like a dead end. But as Violet said, it was better than a poke in the eye.

When they got to the truck, he snapped the car seat in place. He started the engine, cranked up the air conditioner, but then turned toward Violet.

"So, trying to be optimistic like you," he said with a smile, "I'd say we had a bit of success today."

His joking made her chuckle. "I'm glad to know I can be of service."

"We now know the office is open a couple of

days a week, and, like you suspected, the shelter is in a hidden location."

"And that eventually someone should answer your email," she added.

"Good point."

Her pretty greenish eyes sparkled with humor. "Of course, you may have to work on being patient waiting on that email. Which could prove difficult."

The fact she was lightening up, teasing him, sent a shot of awareness through him. Awareness at how beautiful she was. How sweet. And helpful.

And beautiful. Definitely beautiful.

"I beg to differ." He forced a serious expression. "I'm a very patient man."

She raised her brows. "Really? Who slapped a baby car seat in his truck all willy-nilly before trying to look online to find out how to do it?"

"Hey, now. Abigail was screeching. And I hate to inform you, but it wasn't impatience that led me to *slap* it in the truck. It was sheer panic."

A short laugh slipped out before she bit her lip, holding it in, and then looked away.

Why couldn't she just let loose? It seemed every time they enjoyed each other's company for a moment, she backed away.

He'd love to get to know her better. "How about lunch?"

"I'm starving. And I did take the whole day off, so there's no hurry to get back."

"Good." A cozy warmth seeped inside him. The same feeling he used to get on the rare occasions he, Remy and his aunt and uncle spent an evening at home together, everyone getting along nicely. Times that made him feel secure… at least until Remy acted out again, and Paul and Edith held him up as an example of a good kid. Making Remy resent him more. Making him fear he couldn't always live up to his aunt's and uncle's expectations.

As always, that fleeting glow of security reminded him how pathetic he was to long for those close relationships. Having a perfect family was an unattainable ideal anyway.

No, he could only depend on himself.

But lunch was the least he could do for the woman who hadn't given up when they'd found the shelter's office closed, who'd encouraged him to investigate further. Thanks to Violet, Jake now had a lead on someone who possibly knew Remy.

He'd give his favorite hammer for one of the ladies at Dotty's Dippity-Do to call him with information on Remy.

"Now, that's the kind of smell a man wants to have hit his nose when he walks into a place."

The aroma of pizza dough and tangy tomato

sauce filled the air as Violet and Jake waited to be seated in a nondescript pizza parlor in a hole-in-the-road town between Atlanta and Appleton.

Glad she'd agreed to come along, she hoped to get to know him better during lunch. To find out more about this man who was in charge of Abigail's care. To make sure he was as dependable as he seemed.

"You don't like the smell of permanent solution, huh?" she asked with a smirk.

"No way. I don't know why women with straight hair want curly hair anyway. And why women with curly hair want straight hair. Men just like it to be clean and silky so we can run our fingers through it."

Violet's face flamed and probably matched the sauce on the pizza at the table beside them. She couldn't look at Jake until her face cooled.

And even then, she couldn't forget the thought of him running his fingers through her hair.

"Come on back," said the hostess. She led them to a booth along the wall, tossed down menus and then hurried away.

"I like my pizza with thick crust and double meat," Jake said. "You?"

"Uh-oh. I like mine thin with veggies." She leaned her chin on her hand and gave him a smart-alecky smile. "I guess you lose."

"Oh, I don't think so." He winked at her. "They sell it by the slice."

His wink made her stomach do a pirouette.

The waitress arrived, and they placed their order. Because the women's restroom was more likely to have a changing table, Violet offered to take Abigail for a diaper change. When she returned, Jake had his cell phone on the table.

"I haven't gotten a response yet from Peace House. I thought maybe I'd email again now that I know more about the shelter."

"Okay." Violet passed the diaper bag back to Jake.

He took Abigail, popped a pacifier in her mouth, then put her in her carrier beside him on the vinyl seat of the booth. "In my original email, I only said I was looking for my cousin, Remy West, who'd given the shelter's address as her last place of residence."

"Then I definitely think you need to mention she left Abigail with you and that you're trying to get hold of her to discuss Remy returning to get her child."

"Yeah, I agree."

As he typed in the text of the email, she watched his big, calloused fingers stumble over the letters, backtrack and then try again.

He had a cut on the back of his hand that was mostly healed and a new, red and tender scrape on one of his knuckles. Various scars marked previous wounds. He'd probably injured himself on the job numerous times, carrying on without giving the nicks, cuts and bruises a moment's notice.

Had he done the same thing with his bruised heart after his parents died? And what about after any women had broken his heart?

"Tell me what you think," he said, handing her the phone.

In the message, he'd explained the situation and then asked Ms. Phillips, the director, to please pass along word to Remy that Jake was worried and wanted her to email or call him.

"Looks good."

"Then let's send it." After hitting the send button, he put the phone in his pocket.

Violet wanted to smooth the little divot of tension from between Jake's eyebrows. "Don't worry. I think she'll answer this time."

The waitress swooped in and delivered two plates covered in the largest slices of pizza she'd ever seen.

"Enjoy," she said. "I'll bring drink refills ASAP."

Abigail had fallen asleep sucking on the pacifier and napped peacefully. Violet put her napkin in her lap and reached for the fork.

Jake reached across the table. "Let's say a blessing."

"Oh. Okay."

He opened his hand, palm side up.

She swallowed and put her hand in his. As

she'd imagined, his was warm and work-roughened. But she didn't mind—only thought it felt strong and capable.

His blessing over their meal included a request for God to reunite Remy and Abigail. A prayer that left tears in her eyes at his heartfelt plea.

With a brief squeeze of her hand, he released her. As he picked up his fork, she noticed he once again looked worried.

"What are you thinking about that's got your brow wrinkled?" she asked.

"You."

Her hand stilled on the fork. "Me?"

"I hope you'll still stand by your word to give me time to locate Remy. At this point, I think we're at the mercy of Ms. Phillips."

Oh. Disappointment slid in to replace the initial thrill that he'd been thinking of her.

She wanted to huff at her silliness. Why had she set herself up for that roller coaster of emotion? "Of course I will. I gave my word."

"Thanks." He resumed eating with gusto. But no sooner had he bitten off a huge bite than Abigail startled and began to fuss.

Attempting to sweet-talk Abigail, Jake spoke in a high-pitched voice while he rocked the carrier.

Impressed, Violet watched as the infant quickly settled and went back to sleep.

She had to admit her opinion of him was

quickly changing. All week she'd sensed a gap between the villain she'd imagined and the man sitting across from her rocking a car seat and talking baby talk. Was she allowing him to sway her? Would she lose her objectivity?

Still, she was pleased—and relieved—to see that Abigail was in good hands.

Having arrived at the middle of her slice of pizza, she put down her fork, picked up the wedge and chomped off a mouthful. The oozing cheese stretched until it pulled apart and the string hit her chin.

Jake snickered. "I love watching you go after that pizza, determined to conquer it. Like you do everything else—no holds barred."

He hadn't seemed so thrilled when she went about buying the pediatric practice. "So you think of that as a positive trait rather than negative?"

He seemed taken aback by her question. "Well, positive for the most part. As long as it's for good, and no one gets hurt in the process. Like today, when you didn't give up after finding the shelter office closed."

At least he didn't mention his aunt and uncle. "Yeah, I'm pretty driven."

"Why is that?"

If only she could throw out something simple, some adversity all teenagers faced that had made her stronger. But no, she had a much more complicated story. A story she never shared. "I had a falling out with my parents late in high school. Struck out on my own after graduation. Put myself through college, worked hard for good grades, got in med school. I had to be driven to make it through that."

"What caused the falling out?" He chugged some sweet iced tea and looked at her with a pleasant expression, as if expecting a typical answer. *Overbearing rules, disapproval of her goals, didn't like her friends.*

What would he say if she told him she'd gotten pregnant, and when she said she wanted to keep the baby, they refused to support her, whisked her away to her aunt and uncle's house in another state and arranged for an adoption?

"Just the regular stuff," she said.

No one outside her hometown knew her secret and she preferred to keep it that way. She'd enjoyed the freedom from people judging her or, worse, the looks of pity.

"Seems to me it would take more than the standard disagreements to cause a total break with someone as important as your mom and dad."

"I was sorry to learn your parents died when you were young. What happened?"

He wiped a napkin over his mouth. "They were killed in a car accident. I was six." His eyes crinkled as he grimaced. "I can't imagine refusing to see my parents over an argument or 'regular stuff.' I'd trade my right arm to have them back."

Shame burned her face. Shame and dread. Because if she and Jake became friends, she would eventually need to tell him the whole truth—how she'd failed everyone who loved and trusted her and then, when faced with the consequences of her mistake, was too weak to stand up to keep her own child. "I'm sorry for your loss. I understand how you must think my behavior ridiculous."

She excused herself to go to the restroom, where she stared at herself in the mirror, pressing a damp paper towel to her cheeks.

Every time she relived those moments, regret nearly ate her alive.

What if she had been brave enough to strike out on her own, deliver the baby and keep him? Would her life be full and happy now?

Violet dabbed the cool cloth to her neck. Took several deep breaths to gather herself. She'd come to lunch to get to know Jake better. But she'd ended up faced with her own baggage.

Being around Abigail was messing with her mind.

Being around Jake was making her feel vulnerable, as if his good opinion mattered.

But she didn't need Jake or his good opinion. She didn't need anyone.

* * *

Jake jolted awake to total quiet. Bolted straight up in bed, looking at the clock. Five-thirty in the morning. Panic sent his heartbeat racing. Was something wrong with Abigail?

He sprinted to her room and stood over the travel crib. Her deep, even breaths left him weak-kneed with relief, his reaction to Abigail sleeping through the night exactly as Violet had said it might be.

Apparently, they'd worn out the little gal with their trip to Atlanta the day before.

Eager to see if Remy had emailed him, he hurried to the kitchen, bypassed the coffeepot and went straight to his laptop.

An email from the shelter director was in his box. Once again, his heart raced. This could be big news.

Clicking on the message, he held his breath.

Dear Mr. West,
At this time, Remy is not willing to share her contact information. However, she gave me permission to pass along this message:
Jake, I appreciate you caring. I'm doing well. But I have no desire for contact since it will be easier on me, and better for the baby, to make a clean break.
Love, Remy

Jake jammed a hand through his hair. *The baby.* Remy hadn't even called Abigail by her name. As if distancing herself from her child.

At this time? Did that mean Ms. Phillips thought Remy would change her mind down the road? Was it a subtle message to be patient and not give up?

This cloak-and-dagger stuff was going to make him crazy.

He needed to talk to Violet. To get her take on the email. Maybe she'd be on her patio having her morning coffee and watching the sunrise.

He stepped outside and, sure enough, she sat in the semi-dark in shorts and a T-shirt…barefoot…leaning over the table, the light from her tablet illuminating her face.

Always busy, always working. As if she felt she couldn't afford to stop.

Or didn't deserve to?

Not wanting to startle her by calling out her name, he stepped into his yard and waved until she caught the movement out of the corner of her eye and looked up.

"Good morning. Can you come over when you get a minute?"

"Sure." She carried her tablet and coffee mug back into her house and then a moment later reappeared wearing flip-flops.

"Hey," he said when she met him in his yard, looking bright-eyed and sunny…beautiful without makeup, even with a little poof on one side of her hair, as if she'd gone straight from bed to her morning routine.

"Good morning."

An awkward silence fell over them. There was something intimate about meeting before dawn in the middle of dewy grass, her hair rumpled from sleep.

He coughed and shoved the thought out of his mind. "Um. I got an email from the director."

"Really? That's great news."

"No, it's not good news. Do you have time to come read it?"

She nodded and followed him inside.

Violet took a seat at the table, tapped the touchpad to wake the laptop and stared at the screen. Her eyebrows drew downward as she read. "I guess this is good news and bad."

He sat beside her, leaning his arms on the table. "Definitely see the bad. How do you see good?"

"Someone responsible knows where Remy is so that means she's probably safe."

"Good point. I got so caught up on Remy wanting a clean break that I didn't think of that."

"But this also confirms her connection to the shelter, which means she has been, maybe still is, a victim of domestic abuse—horrific to consider." Violet looked away from the screen and put on her serious doctor look. "And, like you said, it confirms Remy doesn't want to come back to get Abigail."

Her stern brow and narrowed eyes raised his hackles. "You promised to give me time. The search isn't over."

"I'm not going to take any action yet. You'll get your time."

He knew that left unsaid was her suspicion that nothing would change during that time.

"Jake, I think you should consider that Remy may be doing the disappearing act to protect Abigail from an abusive father."

"She said he died."

"Maybe that was to keep you from searching for a birth father."

He stood and paced across the kitchen. This would all be a bit easier to swallow with a shot of caffeine.

He grabbed the bag of ground coffee beans. "She seemed different when she was here. I'd like to take her at her word."

"Desperation will make a person say *anything*—even an outright lie." A flush pinkened her cheeks, then her gaze dropped to the table.

Had she lied to him? From the guilty avoiding of eye contact, he couldn't help but suspect she had, maybe in all the hedging she'd done yesterday about her past. Or if not outright lying, maybe hiding something.

Once the coffee and water were in the chamber, he jammed the pot in place and hit the button. "I'm not going to drop the search. I'm going to keep the connection open through the shelter director." He turned and stared into her pretty eyes.

Greenish-brown eyes that looked so innocent and caring didn't necessarily mean she knew best in Abigail's situation.

Regret filled those same eyes. "Fine, continue the search. But I think it may be time for you to contact your lawyer. If nothing else, maybe he or she could help locate Remy."

Violet closed the laptop. She sat perched on the edge of her chair as if expecting him to send her away.

Why, when she looked so vulnerable, did it eat at him? Make him feel like a big, jerky clod?

With an irritated huff, he went to get two cups of coffee out of the machine before it was done brewing. Dripping coffee sizzled on the warmer as he quickly poured them.

"Well, you've stated your opinion. But I'm willing to wait a little longer to give Remy a chance. If she's off the drugs, I know she'll come back."

He sure hoped he was making the right decision and wasn't just acting out of fear of having a baby thrust into his life.

"I'm sorry, Jake. I know this is a complicated

family matter for you and your cousin. I'm just trying to focus on Abigail's welfare."

"So am I. So, ultimately, we're on the same side."

"You're doing a good job," she said.

"Only because you've shown me everything I know about caring for a baby." He gave her a grateful smile, glad they'd both shared their opinions without anyone storming out. Simone, the last woman he'd dated, had loved drama. And of course, he'd grown up with Remy's rebellious behavior, which kept the household in an uproar most of the time.

He placed a mug in front of her. "I'm sorry I don't have cream. How about sugar?"

"Black will be fine." She held the mug with two hands as if warming them. Then she took a sip. Her eyes darted to his over the rim and his gaze locked with hers. Once again, he felt an odd sense of intimacy. This time over having morning coffee together.

He must be sleep deprived.

After a few more drinks of the brew, she stood. "I'm sorry to rush off. I have a patient to check on at the hospital this morning. Will you work today?"

"Working from home again. Zeb's keeping me updated. I plan to make an announcement at church tomorrow asking for help with child care."

She went to the sink, rinsed her mug and placed it in the dishwasher. "I hope someone comes forward. In the meantime, I could come this afternoon if you want a few hours to go to the job site."

"You'd do that again?"

"Sure. I close at noon on Saturday."

"Then yes, I'd appreciate that. As payment, I'll bring carryout home with me and feed you dinner."

With arms crossed in front of her, she clutched her elbows, looking tense, nervous. "How about I make dinner? I love to cook and rarely take the time for just myself."

Surprised, he eyed her. "After babysitting all afternoon, why would you do that for me?"

"Because…I love to cook?" She laughed, and some of the earlier tension left the room.

He sure loved to hear her laugh. He leaned back, crossed his arms over his chest and decided to tease her a little. "Doc, why spend a Saturday evening with me and a baby when you could invite some nice man over and cook for him, like a real date?"

"Well, now, that would be rude of me since I already invited you. Of course, if you decline…"

He barked a laugh. "No, I'm not declining. A good home-cooked meal sounds amazing. I admit, I'm seriously wondering your angle."

"Quit trying to figure me out." Her smooth cheeks turned pink. "If I offer, and you want to accept, then accept. Don't get caught up in motivations."

The problem was, they both seemed to have complicated motivations. And it was going to drive him up the wall trying to figure out hers. He needed to stick with the facts.

The fact was, she was willing to help him with Abigail...for now.

"I've been thinking," he said. "I might send Remy some photos of Abigail, hoping it'll make her want to come home."

Pain sliced across Violet's expression. Was she sympathizing with Remy?

"I guess it couldn't hurt to try," Violet said. "But Remy told you a break in contact would be easier on her."

"I'm not trying to make it easy on Remy. I'm trying to reunite Abigail with her mother."

And he wouldn't quit trying to do that, even if he was finding he enjoyed Abigail more each day.

Even if giving up the baby would end time together with Violet.

Chapter Six

Tired of jogging clothes and work clothes, and determined to look a bit more feminine, Violet loaded Abigail into the car as soon as Jake left for work that afternoon. She headed to Chloe's Closet.

"Come on, Abigail," she said as they entered the store with a jingle of bells. "Come see the fun clothes and accessories that lie in your future."

"I'll be with you in a minute," Chloe O'Malley called from somewhere in the back of the shop.

Fall clothes filled the display at the front, the first items for the change of season, which was still a couple of months away.

One wall was lined with candles and cute, creative items for the home. Scattered about were racks of costume jewelry and handbags.

Back in her teens, Violet had shopped at boutiques like this, where they stocked only one or two items in each size. Her mother had bought her fine clothes…anything Violet wanted.

Now, with her business building so slowly in addition to student loans, she had a limited budget. Time to search the sale rack.

"Oh, hi, Violet. What can I help you with today?"

She lifted the carrier so Chloe could see the baby. "I'm sitting again but thought I'd drop by and see if Abigail will cooperate while I try on a few things."

"Oh, I'll be delighted to help. What are you looking for?"

"Something casual, comfortable. But nicer than my work clothes." Violet looked down at her black slacks and utilitarian white blouse. "A little color might be nice."

"Do you have a date?" Chloe's silvery-blue eyes twinkled. "Maybe an outing with the baby and then a date with the hunky guardian?"

Violet's face blasted like a raging fever. "I'm simply cooking dinner for him. Not a date at all. Just neighbors getting together."

Except if she were totally honest, she'd have to admit she hoped for more.

"I see." Chloe stifled a laugh as she sorted through the rack and pulled out a slinky red dress.

"No way. That screams that I'm trying too hard."

"It's cotton knit, so it's very comfortable and casual."

Not casual in Violet's book. "My type of comfortable is running shorts and a T-shirt. That dress shouts, 'Look at me!'"

"What's wrong with making a man notice?"

She gave Chloe a look that said *move on*.

"Okay." Chloe flipped through several more hangers. Then she pulled out another dress. It was long and had spaghetti straps.

"Nope. How about pants and a knit top?"

With a sigh, Chloe went around to the other side of the rack. "Chicken."

Yeah. She was. But she wasn't trying to attract Jake. She just wanted to look nice.

Nice enough to make him take notice?

"You know, never mind. I don't know what I was thinking." She lugged the carrier toward the exit. "I'm sorry for wasting your time."

"No, don't leave," Chloe called, rushing to block her path. "I'm sorry. I'm a little too into playing matchmaker since my sister, Darcy, had me do a makeover for her."

"I heard she got engaged. So I guess the makeover did the trick."

Chloe let out a peal of laughter. "Actually, the date that night was with another man. But Mr. Right won out."

While Violet tried to figure out that comment, Chloe took the baby seat from her. "Come on. I'll watch Abigail while you pick something *you* like."

Trying to relax and enjoy the search, Violet took her time selecting several items and then tried them on. After Chloe weighed in with her opinion, Violet settled on a long, straight blue knit skirt and a casual top with a green, blue and white geometric pattern. As she was checking out, she spotted a cute pair of sandals on the clearance rack.

"Perfect," Chloe said. "You'll look great and feel great in that outfit."

"I hope so." A nervous tangle of butterflies sent her stomach on a nosedive as she thought of spending the evening with Jake over a nice, quiet dinner. But what if he didn't even notice her new outfit?

What if he did?

Snapping her attention back to Chloe, Violet punched in the PIN for her debit card. "I appreciate your help. Now...on to the grocery store."

Chloe handed a shopping bag across the counter, the new clothes nicely wrapped in tissue paper. "I have a feeling you and Jake will have a wonderful evening. I'll be praying that you do."

This woman she barely knew would be praying for her? Touched, Violet felt grateful for her new friendships here in Appleton. Maybe she was making a place for herself in town after all.

Barely able to thank Chloe because of the

lump in her throat, Violet said goodbye and left the shop.

Had God brought her here and blessed her with this community? Would He do that despite the fact she'd shut Him out for more than a decade?

She couldn't imagine that God cared that much. Yet some part of her deep inside, the little-girl part that had loved Sunday school and vacation Bible school and singing "Jesus Loves Me" at the top of her lungs, hoped so. That teenaged mother who felt crushed and empty when she had to leave her son behind in Alabama wanted to believe God could still love her.

Grief nearly overwhelmed Violet as she purchased the ingredients for dinner. The only thing that helped her pull herself together was Abigail's need for attention.

She had a job to do. She could focus on that.

But when she pulled up in front of Jake's beautiful bungalow and realized she felt instantly at home, her eyes stung with tears. The knot reformed in her throat. Ever since the hairstylist had complimented them on their family of three, she'd had to battle picturing them that way. Battle the thrill the comment gave her.

Abigail whimpered.

Time to forget her silly emotions and take care of the baby. Pushing away thoughts of families and excitement over having dinner with Jake, she carried the groceries and Abigail inside.

She quickly put away the food and then prepared a bottle. The tiny girl happily drank her formula. Heavy-lidded eyes looked at Violet as the eating slowed.

"Shopping can wear a girl out," she whispered. Pressing her cheek to the baby's soft head, she inhaled. She hadn't been allowed to hold her baby boy. When she'd held other babies through the years, she'd often tried to imagine his scent. Longing tugged at her insides, and she had to tamp it down. Tamp it back into the safe prison it had been in for years.

Once Abigail finished eating, Violet strapped on the soft baby carrier and slipped her inside, against her chest. She walked over to her own house, grabbed a few food staples and cooking utensils, loaded them in a large tote, then carried them back to Jake's.

Violet needed to start dinner. She lifted Abigail, now wide-awake, out of the carrier and put her in the bouncy seat.

"Time to cook for your dad—I mean cousin." She shook her head, irritated at the direction her traitorous thoughts kept going.

Stepping out of her fantasy world, she focused on cooking the best rosemary chicken she'd ever made. The most buttery roasted vegetables. The creamiest mashed potatoes.

As she prepared the food, she talked to Abigail and bounced the seat to keep her entertained. While the chicken baked, Violet bathed the baby. Then she fed her again and put her down in the baby bed.

Jake texted to say he was on the way home, so she hurriedly cleaned up and changed into her new clothes. She was setting the table when she heard the front door creak open.

"I'm home," Jake called, his deep voice making her heart skip a beat. Anticipation sent her stomach flying as if she'd reached the highest point of a Ferris wheel.

Lord, help me.

The automatic plea startled her. Though it had been years, the cry for divine help had come naturally. Maybe the fact Chloe was praying had affected her.

Or maybe her growing feelings for Jake and Abigail left her desperate for God to protect her heart.

Lord, I know it's been ages. But I need Your help, and quickly. I have so much baggage. I have no business feeling like this about Jake. He doesn't know my past, and for some reason, I'm scared to tell him.

And while You're listening—assuming You are—Jake and Remy need Your help, too. Please help them find the best solution for Abigail.

"Man, something sure smells good." Jake

stepped into the kitchen. Once again, he brought in the smell of sawdust and sunshine, a smell she would forever associate with him.

He whistled.

Her heart stilled. "I'm glad you appreciate a good home-cooked meal."

His eyes took her in from head to toe and back. "That's not all I appreciate. I was talking about you, Violet. You look beautiful."

The way he said her name with his deep, masculine voice left her breathless as she looked into his eyes. "Thank you."

"New outfit?"

"Yes, Abigail and I went shopping."

He chuckled. "Well, the kid's got good taste. She helped you pick a winner." His eyes shone with admiration.

Exactly the look she'd secretly hoped to see on his face.

She turned toward the stove. "Abigail's asleep, and dinner's ready."

"Great. I'll run back to check on her and wash up."

While he was gone, she busied herself putting food on the table. When she heard his footsteps returning, she pressed her hands against her stomach, trying to calm her nerves.

"She's sleeping soundly," he said when he returned. "How'd my girl do for you?"

My girl. The tender endearment shot straight

to her heart because she could so see him as a father...as a husband.

Lord, please help... "Abigail's been great. She hung out in the bouncy seat as I cooked."

"Food looks amazing."

"Have a seat."

He held out a chair for her, which was very gentlemanly—and maybe date-like?—and made her feel special.

He went around to the other side of the table. This time she knew to wait for the blessing.

After he prayed, he put his napkin in his lap. "Thanks for all this."

He smiled, looking into her eyes, and the connection soothed some of her nervousness and fear. He was a good man who could be her friend. As long as she didn't get caught up in old hopes and dreams.

"Everything is delicious," he said. "My aunt used to make a similar chicken dish, but I haven't had it in ages."

"I'm glad you like it. I've wondered...were you and Remy close as children?"

"We've had a love–hate relationship."

"How's that?"

He stirred the sauce spilling off the chicken with his fork, as if deep in thought. After a moment, he looked up. "She resented me intruding into her world. An only child suddenly sharing her parents."

"I imagine you were in a bad place, too."

"Yeah. Shocked and grieving the loss of my parents. Uprooted from my home and friends. Paul and Edith were kind to take me in. They tried to treat me like one of their own."

"But Remy didn't like that."

He shook his head. "I was six, and she wasn't quite eight."

"Oh, wow. I'd assumed she's younger than you."

"Paul and Edith were older when she was born, so they'd spoiled her. I came in and ruined that. When she started complaining and acting out, I was afraid they'd send me away."

"You poor thing. Did you two ever get along?"

"By the time we were in middle and high school, my aunt and uncle worked long hours. Remy rebelled as a way to lash out at them. And me."

She passed him the bowl of potatoes for a second helping. "So the two of you were on your own a lot?"

He grimaced. "Yeah. Now, enough about me. What about you? Any siblings?"

"Nope. I'm an only child."

"Were you close to your parents before the falling out?"

She did not want to get into her past. She already knew how one question could lead to another. "Not really. Did you and Remy ever grow close?"

"Nice job dodging talking about yourself."

"I want you to finish the story of you and Remy."

He heaved a sigh. "I tried to keep her out of trouble. We even had moments of closeness as we bonded over being alone for dinner." With an ironic laugh, he shook his head. "I'd make her favorite foods, hoping she'd stay home instead of going out to parties."

"Sounds like you cared about her."

"Yeah. Feeding her was a peace offering."

Violet's chest tightened, feeling pain for this boy who'd already lost so much. She couldn't resist touching him, putting her hand over his. "You didn't owe her a peace offering, you know. You were just a hurting kid, too."

He glanced up from his plate, his expression pure agony. "Still, that's how she felt. She blamed me for being 'the good child' trying to take her parents' affection, when I was actually being good so they didn't ship me back into foster care."

Swallowing against tears for a young Jake, she waited for him to finish.

"Remy ended up addicted to drugs and ran away. I failed her."

"No, you didn't. Any decision to use drugs was hers."

He leaned forward, determination sparking in his eyes. "I need to keep my promise to Remy. I won't let Abigail down."

Ever since high school, when Hank had deserted her and her parents had let *her* down, Violet had had trust issues. But at the moment, she wanted to believe Jake was someone she could trust. Someone she could maybe let herself care about.

So far, he'd proven himself dependable with Abigail. He needed to be assured of that.

Feeling bad for dredging up hurtful memories, she also wanted to lighten the moment. "Jake, you're doing a fantastic job with Abigail. For a rookie."

When he jerked his gaze to hers, she smiled to let him know she was teasing.

"A rookie, huh?"

"Yep. For a man who'd never changed a diaper, you've really taken to this fathering gig. I'm impressed."

The pain in his eyes cleared, and a sigh slipped out. "I'm determined not to fail Remy again."

No wonder he didn't want to give up the hunt for Remy and contact the lawyer. "I totally get that now."

Setting his napkin on the table, he stared into her eyes. "Good, I'm glad."

In that moment, she felt a closeness to this man she'd never experienced with anyone before.

He'd opened up to her, shared about his family, exposed his pain. Pain that lived with him still.

Maybe someday, she could be as brave.

Yet she needed to be careful. It was going to be more difficult than ever not to get drawn in by this kind, caring man who'd been loyal to his cousin despite his own hurt. Who'd tried his best to take care of her and still worried about her.

A man who was willing to step up and watch over Abigail.

An honorable man who wasn't anything like she'd thought.

Last night had gotten entirely too cozy.

Jake set aside the ridiculous bond he'd felt with Violet over dinner the previous evening. Sure, she lived nearby. Sure, she'd helped him. But he had to use the good sense God had given him.

He didn't need to get entangled with a woman who hadn't let him past her defenses despite the fact he'd dumped his emotional baggage out onto the table last night.

Every time he'd tried to turn the conversation to her family, she managed a slick move to avoid the topic, leaving him feeling as if he'd said too much.

Vulnerable was not a good place to be.

He hefted Abigail's car seat into the pew and took his place for the Sunday morning service.

Today, he would announce that he needed a babysitter. Surely he would find someone to replace Violet. Who could resist a sweet little thing like Abigail?

As the organ started playing, Violet slipped in the other end of the pew wearing a knee-length skirt and sleeveless red sweater. She glanced timidly his way as she parked herself right by the outside aisle, the same place she'd been last week when they'd both been too stubborn to acknowledge each other with much more than a nod. He should probably invite her to scoot over next to them, yet he hesitated.

Once settled, she smiled and waved.

He did the same and immediately felt guilty for not being a more inviting, friendlier church member.

What was wrong with him? It wasn't as if asking her to slide fifteen feet closer was an invitation to spend her life with him. Yet, still, he balked.

Would it be more difficult to find a babysitter if everyone thought he and Violet were together? It could. Some women wouldn't want to butt into another woman's territory.

Just thinking such things made his chest clench. He glanced over. Violet looked lovely with colored light from the stained glass window beaming on her shiny ebony hair and smooth, pale shoulder. Lovely, yet so alone at the end of the pew. She had only begun attending church, had come twice now and must feel a little anxious about being new.

As the hymn ended—with him hardly singing a word—he placed the hymnal in the rack in front of him and leaned over to catch her attention.

When she finally looked at him, he waved her over. *Join us?* he mouthed, pointing to the place beside Abigail's seat.

She gave him a tentative smile and reached for her purse. While the pastor made announcements for the upcoming week, she settled next to Abigail and gently brushed her hand over the baby's head.

"Does anyone else have an announcement to share?" Ted Greer asked.

Time for him to take that step so he wouldn't be dependent on Violet. Jake raised his hand and stood. "I do, although it's more of a request."

Glancing around the sanctuary, Jake took in the smiles and curious gazes. "Some of you may know that my cousin, Remy, had a baby. She recently left the baby in my care while she gets her life straightened out."

Whispers sounded around the sanctuary.

"As you can imagine, I've needed help learning how to take care of a three-week-old baby." A few people chuckled in response. "The new pediatrician, who's started attending here, has been a huge help." He looked at her and nodded his thanks.

"But Violet is busy with her patients, and I'm looking to hire someone to babysit. I can be flexible on the hours. Please talk to me after church if you're willing or interested."

Violet smiled at him as he sat back down, but her eyes looked large and sad, almost wounded.

What's wrong? he mouthed as the pastor called on Grace Hunt to make another announcement.

She shook her head, mouthed, *Nothing,* and then turned her attention to Grace.

He had to take her at her word. But those expressive eyes nudged at him through the rest of the worship service.

Irritated, he trained his full attention on the pulpit. He needed to focus on finding Remy and taking care of Abigail. Not worry about the hurt in Violet's eyes.

As soon as Pastor Greer dismissed the congregation, Violet stood and reached for her purse. Before Jake could speak to her, Abigail, who'd slept the past hour, started cranking up to a good cry. As he unbuckled her from the carrier, someone touched his arm.

He glanced back. Two women stood nearby, fussing over the baby.

Kelli Calhoun, the college student Grace had mentioned on the phone last week, said, "I'm available to babysit three afternoons a week. Could sure use the income."

He whipped back around to pick up his crying cousin but found Violet getting her out of the seat.

"Do you have babysitting experience?" Jake asked.

"Lots."

"Can you write down your info, uh…" He patted his pockets. No business cards.

"I'll write it on my bulletin," she said, reaching for a pencil in a holder on the back of the pew.

"I'll add my contact info, as well," said Liza, a young, frazzled single mother of four who lived just outside of town. She touched his shoulder and leaned against him as she admired Abigail. "I've always got room for one more precious baby."

Liza's youngest was maybe six months old. Jake couldn't see her taking on a three-week-old. That and her overfamiliarity set off a warning, making his decision. Putting space between them, he thanked her for the offer. An offer he wouldn't accept.

When he turned to check on Abigail, he found Violet sitting with her, feeding her a bottle. He smiled his thanks, but she seemed distracted, looking everywhere but at him.

Someone placed a hand on his back.

Simone Peters gave him a sulky look, her dark, mysterious eyes trying to shame him. "I can't believe you didn't call me. I would have come to your rescue."

He'd broken up with Simone a year ago when she started hinting at marriage and a huge mortgage, and never in a million years would he have thought to ask her to babysit. She was not the motherly type.

She wrapped her arm around his and held tight to his biceps, her cloyingly sweet fragrance overpowering him. "I'm available anytime you need me. You have my number." The deep husky voice that had once attracted him now seemed fake, forced.

Fighting the urge to pinch his nose shut against her perfume, he removed himself from her clutches. "Thanks, Simone. I'll keep that in mind."

"Can I hold the poor, sweet thing?" Simone squeezed in the pew, making sure she brushed against him as she squeezed by, then turned her attention to Abigail. "Oh, I just love babies."

Since when? "She's eating right now."

"I don't mind taking over." Simone slid one arm under Abigail and took hold of the bottle.

Violet narrowed her eyes at Simone as she lifted the baby.

Ahhh. Maybe Violet's hurt look during announcements had something to do with becoming attached to Abigail. Despite going along with Jake's plan, maybe she hated to turn over care to someone else. Admittedly, the thought pleased him.

No, he had to consider his work schedule. Had to get back to business as usual—finishing up the Emerson house and other projects.

"Oh, she's adorable." Simone snuggled Abigail and kissed her forehead.

Never would he have thought… "I didn't know you had any experience with babies."

"I used to babysit my nephew." She smiled proudly, then promptly passed Abigail to Jake rather than back to Violet.

Before she tried to squeeze past him again, he moved into the aisle. "Simone, Violet, have you two met?"

"No, I don't believe we've had the pleasure," Simone said, holding out her hand.

Violet stood and shook. "Nice to meet you."

Simone looked from Violet to him and back. "It was so nice of you to help Jake."

Violet scooted next to him, touching her shoulder against his. She smiled up at him sweetly, and humor sparked in her eyes. "Oh, I haven't minded."

Tension rippled in the air. Jake might be a clueless guy, but even he could sense Simone's claws popping out.

"Well, Violet, you can rest assured that help

has arrived. I'm on vacation for the next week, and since Jake's and my annual scuba diving trip got canceled, I'm free."

Jake's and my? Jake had backed out of their annual trip—with a large group of friends—last year after their breakup.

"I'm serious, Jake. Call me." Simone gave Violet a quick smile, then sauntered toward the door.

"Well, that was interesting," Violet said.

He bit back a smile. Simone could be a lot to take in for a newcomer. "She's a handful."

"I'm sorry, but I didn't care for the way she barged in without considering the baby's need to eat peacefully."

"Feeling a little territorial where Abigail's concerned?"

"Of course not." Flustered, Violet leaned over and grabbed her purse. The contents dumped on the floor.

"Here, I'll help."

"No, thanks. I've got it." She struggled to put everything back. Peeked at her phone.

"I'm pleased by the response for babysitting help," Jake said. "What did you think about the candidates?"

Pinning him with her gaze, she raised her brows. "I think maybe a couple of them were offering more than babysitting services. But Kelli seemed promising."

Jake barked a laugh, causing Violet's irritated expression to soften.

"Hey, you two." Chloe O'Malley approached and brushed a finger over Abigail's cheek. "If you ask me, Violet's the perfect babysitter. And I don't have much free time. But if you get in a jam, call me. Between me, my mom and Darcy, one of us should be able to cover for you."

"Thanks, Chloe."

She gave Violet a smile and then walked away.

Violet sighed. "I need to check on a newborn in the hospital. Remember, if you value your own safety, hire that sweet girl Kelli."

He couldn't help but grin as she went to greet the pastor and then slipped outside.

As the door shut behind her, it hit him that he wouldn't see much of Violet now unless Abigail needed to see a doctor. He felt as if he'd lost something important.

Abigail spit out the bottle. He lifted her to his shoulder for a burp. "I guess the two of us need to learn to make our way without Violet."

He couldn't get soft because Violet was growing attached to Abigail…or because he was growing attached to both of them.

Time to get back on task.

Searching the sanctuary, he found Kelli talking to a cluster of friends. He hurried over to catch her as she was leaving. "Kelli, hold up."

She stopped.

"Which days do you have available to babysit?"

"Monday, Wednesday and Friday afternoons."

"Have you got references?"

"Yeah. I've worked in the nursery, so ask Pastor Ted. And I've babysat for Miss Liza's kids. She'll vouch for me."

"You're hired. I'll check your references, but if you don't hear from me otherwise, plan on starting tomorrow."

"Thanks, Jake! I won't let you down. Tomorrow at one?"

He'd prefer mornings, but she was his only option at the moment. "Yeah. Thanks."

As he went back to the pew to put Abigail in her car seat, he thought of Violet plastering herself up against him while defending him against Simone. More than once, Jake had been blindsided by the cozy feeling that seemed to surround the three of them when he, Violet and Abigail were together. But that bond wasn't permanent, wasn't real.

What was real was the fact that he needed to find Remy and reclaim his normal life. And he hoped to accomplish that by sending her photos of Abigail.

Violet tried to dodge well-meaning church members who greeted her as she left the building.

She needed to get out of there. Without showing her hurt. And without going after either of the women who'd *volunteered*—more like fallen all over themselves—to babysit because they obviously wanted to sink their claws into Jake.

Angry over her own petty jealousy, Violet hurried to her car. It wasn't her business whom Jake decided to date. Or whom he decided to hire—as long as Abigail was in good hands.

Violet should celebrate that he now had child-care options that left her free to focus on growing her practice. The timing was perfect because she'd just learned she'd been approved to teach parenting classes at the hospital. Plus, she'd been invited by the local elementary school's parent–teacher organization to speak to parents and their kids about nutrition and exercise. Both engagements would help her meet potential new patient families.

Then why did her stomach and heart ache?

It was time to step back from the West family.

Jake had been doing an excellent job of caring for Abigail. He didn't need her anymore. Her job was done.

"Violet, dear, wait up."

She found Grace Hunt following her through the parking lot. The woman, probably near seventy, looked much younger and moved like a fifty-year-old.

Grace smiled as she approached. "You sure were moving at a clip, young lady."

"I'm sorry. I didn't see you."

Grace gave Violet's hand a squeeze. "I'm sorry my schedule won't allow me to help Jake with Abigail right now. I'm thankful you were there to support him. The two of you, along with Abigail, look good together. You should stake your claim."

Violet's breath hitched. "Excuse me?"

Grace's kind eyes told her more than words could. "You're available, he's available. And you seem to get along well. I think you should go for it."

Go for it. Violet found herself fighting a nervous laugh. The woman was too perceptive for comfort and probably wouldn't accept a denial. "There's more to the situation than you know."

"Doesn't matter. You three look good together, like a ready-made family."

Pain needled its way into her chest. "Besides the fact Jake has no interest in me, I'm not looking to marry and have kids. I'm fulfilled taking care of the children in my practice."

Grace looked away, waved. "Oh, there's Jake now."

With a gasp, Violet turned to see if he'd heard the conversation. He was right behind her. She couldn't be certain.

"Hey, you two," he said with a smile. A big smile.

Violet found it difficult to make eye contact. Had he heard Grace playing matchmaker? "Hey."

"Violet, I wanted to catch you," he said, "to let you know you're definitely off the hook. If Kelli's references check out, and I'm sure they will, she's starting tomorrow."

"Oh, that's great." Her gaze darted to Grace.

Grace's eyes narrowed, and she gave a tiny, almost imperceptible nod, as if urging Violet to stake that claim. Then she turned to Jake. "That's nice of Kelli. So it'll fit around her classes?"

"Yes. Now I need to find someone to cover mornings."

"Simone?" Violet couldn't resist asking.

His lip twitched. "I may have to."

"Or Violet," Grace said with a grin.

Jake seemed surprised by her suggestion. "She has patients to see."

"Jake's right, Grace. Patient numbers have been dropping." She widened her eyes at him, placing the blame. "I need to spend more time out in the community, getting my name out there."

Abigail, who'd been sitting quietly in her carrier in Jake's strong hands, started to fuss. Violet fought the urge to reach for her.

What if Kelli wasn't reliable? Wasn't capable? What if Jake was forced to use Simone?

What if Simone's hideous perfume was toxic? Surely any fragrance by the gallon would be.

"Does Kelli have experience with a baby so young?" Violet had to ask to try to put her mind at ease.

"Well, I didn't ask for specifics." His eyes clouded. "But she's worked in the church nursery. That would cover all ages."

"Be sure to check with the pastor. And watch closely tomorrow to see how Kelli handles Abigail."

Grace nodded approval, a small smile on her face.

"Will do," he said. "I've gotta run. I'll see you ladies around."

As he strode toward his truck, Grace put a hand on Violet's arm. "I know it's early, but I see how you two look at each other. Don't be afraid to follow your heart."

Afraid? More like scared to death that I'm going to fall for Jake and this child.

"Grace, you're sweet to worry about me. I assure you, I'm happy with my life."

And she was. She had new opportunities that lay ahead, opportunities for getting to know townspeople, to prove she was a good person, a good doctor.

Yes, she would stake her claim. Not with a man, but with her career, the only thing she'd ever been able to depend on.

Chapter Seven

Jake walked into Violet's office building carrying Abigail and lunch, his stomach tense.

Today would be a big step. This afternoon, Abigail would have her first day with a regular babysitter so Jake could go back to work—if not full-time, then at least on a better schedule.

Yet a sense of unease hung over him.

What if Kelli wasn't as attentive as he'd like? Did she know infant CPR? If Abigail cried, would Kelli be patient?

Jake shook off the pointless worry. Just inside the door, he walked up to the patient sign-in window. Was that... "Hillary?"

His aunt and uncle's longtime receptionist looked up and then broke into a grin. "Well, will you look who's here? Haul yourself back here so I can hug your neck."

Jake cut through the waiting room and entered the front office. Hillary was waiting with open arms.

He hugged her and kissed her cheek. "So good to see you."

"You, too. And is this Remy's baby I've been hearing about?"

He proudly lifted the carrier. "Yep. Meet Abigail."

Hillary bent over to inspect the baby, to rub her head and pat her cheek. "Oh, she's beautiful! Looks just like Remy."

"Yeah, that's what I think, too."

She reached out and patted his cheek as she had Abigail's, the same way she'd always done when he'd come to the office as a child. "It's good to see you, Jake."

"You, too. I didn't realize you were working here or I would have dropped by during regular hours. I thought Violet let all the employees go."

"No, that's the rumor that went around. She actually just asked us all to reapply for our positions and opened up the job search to get the best people. I didn't do it at first. Thought I might retire, but I quickly got bored. I've only been back working for a few weeks."

Once again, he'd misjudged Violet. He needed to undo the damage he'd caused by voicing his doubt about her around town.

"I'm glad you're back, Hillary. Violet's lucky to have you."

"What brings you by? Is the baby sick?"

His neck heated. "Brought a thank-you lunch for Violet." He lifted the bag in front of him. "There are probably enough sandwiches for you, as well."

"Thank you, dear. I would get her, but—"

The phone rang. Hillary held up her finger and reached for the receiver.

"Appleton Pediatrics."

Jake placed Abigail's seat on the floor and wheeled over an extra chair.

"She's with patients and can't come to the phone right now," Hillary said into the phone. "Can I take a message?"

Her brows drew downward, and she bit her lip as she listened. "I'm sorry. I can take the information again." She flipped open the message log and wrote as the caller dictated.

"Yes, ma'am. I'll make sure she gets this."

She paused, nodded. "I'm certain I did pass it along last time."

Hillary gave him a sad look as she listened to the caller.

"Okay. I promise." She hung up and shook her head. "I know it's not any of my business, but Violet's poor mother keeps calling, week after week."

Jake's heart dropped. Her mother was trying to repair the relationship? Violet hadn't mentioned that. "And she doesn't call her mother back?"

"Not that I can gather. But again, it's none of my business." She straightened and sucked in a deep breath. "So, you brought lunch?"

He handed her the bag. "It needs to be refrigerated until y'all have a chance to eat."

"I'll run it to the break room now. Don't leave. I want to visit a little longer."

"Wish I could, but I have a babysitter coming soon. Need to get back to the house."

"I'm glad you dropped by. Don't be a stranger." She gave him a quick hug as a patient entered the front door. She greeted the patient as he headed out.

Was stubborn pride keeping Violet from calling her parents? He didn't know the details of the family dynamics. Maybe they were a negative force in her life.

As he drove home, he remembered Hillary writing down a phone number in the message book. Did the parents have a different phone number from the one Violet grew up with? Or was the mother afraid Violet wouldn't remember?

The thought caused an ache in his chest. For Violet. For her parents.

When he and Abigail arrived at the house, a small, beat-up sedan sat outside. Kelli climbed out, looking like a typical college student who had rolled out of bed and gone straight to class: blond hair pulled into a loose ponytail, no makeup, outfit of loose-fitting workout clothes that resembled pajamas.

He parked and retrieved the baby seat from the back. "You're early."

"My last class got canceled, so I thought I'd come on over to get familiar with the baby and her schedule."

Smart girl had just earned bonus points in addition to the good references the pastor and other employer had given her. "I appreciate it. Come on in."

He took her inside and showed her around. While he was explaining Abigail's schedule, Kelli checked her vibrating cell phone at least four times. He clenched his teeth to keep from saying something rude.

"I'm sorry," she said. "I forgot to tell my mom and my boyfriend where I would be this afternoon."

Boyfriend? "I'm afraid I can't allow your boyfriend to come over while you're babysitting."

Instead of answering him immediately, she glanced at her phone screen once more. "No problem."

Avoiding eye contact? "No friends over at all. I need your full attention focused on the baby."

"Definitely," she said as she shoved her phone in her back pocket and gave him a big smile.

He felt marginally better. "Okay, I've written

down a feeding schedule that I'll keep on the refrigerator. Do you know how to make bottles?"

"Yep. I've been babysitting since I was fourteen."

"Ever watched one this young?"

"Well, no. But I do watch a six-month-old. For the little ones, I know about burping after feeding, supporting her head, putting her on her back to sleep and all that."

Jake wanted to groan out loud. There was a big difference between a three-week-old and a six-month-old. "It's time for Abigail to have a bottle. How about you make it, and I'll watch?"

A hint of irritation flashed in her eyes. "Sure." He could imagine the eye roll that might have gone along with her agreement if he hadn't been looking.

And he was looking. Closely. This was his— Remy's—baby they were talking about.

Kelli did a decent job making the bottle. It wasn't exactly as he usually did it, but it was good enough.

"Ta-da!" she said when it was ready. "You want me to do the honors?"

"Please."

Jake handed over Abigail, and it was like handing off a piece of himself into the big bad world. Abigail had certainly taken over a corner of his heart.

Kelli carried the baby to the living room and

sat on the couch. She did a perfectly fine job of feeding her.

So why did he feel so unsettled?

Kelli put Abigail on her shoulder and patted. When she coaxed a burp out of Abigail, she smiled at him. "We're good if you want to go."

"My phone number's in the kitchen on the counter. And of course you know to dial 911 if you have any sort of emergency—like choking or a head injury or—"

"I know." She laughed. "You're as bad as my sister after she had her first baby."

Yes, he was being ridiculous. Yet he hadn't felt this worry at all with Violet. "Call if you need me."

He forced himself out the door, then climbed into the truck and slammed the door. Time to go to work and let Kelli do her job.

When he arrived at the work site, Zeb came out and shook his hand. "How'd Friday go?"

"Made a little progress. Made a connection to someone who knows where Remy is and found out she's fine."

"That's good."

"Wood floors getting laid?"

"Yep. Started late this morning."

"Thanks." He nodded and headed inside.

The kitchen looked good. Jake had directed them to repaint in a lighter color, which helped the owner accept the tile she'd ordered and then tried to reject. Last he'd heard, she was happy with the lighter shade of yellow, even if she wasn't happy that he'd been away, taking care of his baby cousin.

He passed through the kitchen, then stuck his head in the large formal dining room. The men, down on their knees with sweat dripping off them, lined up bamboo boards and malleted them in place. "Looks good. Any problems?"

"Hi, Jake. Going smoothly. Should be done early."

"I like the sound of that."

As he headed to the garage, his phone vibrated. He quickly yanked it out.

Thankfully, it wasn't Kelli. It was the homeowner, waffling about the refrigerator he'd already ordered for her.

He explained about the custom cabinets they'd already installed to fit the original. Talked her off the ledge. Made her fall in love once again with the one that would be delivered that week.

Something made a noise outside. Sounded almost like a baby.

He stalked out of the garage. Surely it wasn't Kelli with Abigail. He'd left the car seat base behind but had instructed her not to drive Abigail anywhere unless it was an emergency.

He looked around the work site. No babies in sight. Must've been some type of vehicle driving by. Or a squalling cat. Either that, or he was losing his mind.

Zeb stepped outside the garage. "You found a permanent babysitter yet?"

"Part-time, yeah. But she's new, and it's tough not to worry."

"Turning into a regular mother hen," Zeb muttered with a grin and shake of his head.

Maybe so. But Jake was the sole person responsible for Abigail and wouldn't apologize.

Had he reminded Kelli to turn on the baby monitor while Abigail napped?

Jake needed to do some paperwork. Make some calls. All jobs that could be done at his home office. "Hey, since it looks like you've got things under control here, I think I'll head to the house."

"Go ahead, Mr. Mom."

The affectionate jab didn't bother Jake as much as he would have thought. He clapped Zeb on the back, then drove home.

He felt bad once he'd pulled into the driveway, though. Kelli's family was well respected in town. He knew her from church. She was a smart kid. And so far, dependable. His returning early might hurt her feelings.

Maybe not if he paid her for the full time period.

He unlocked the front door and stepped inside. "I'm back."

Kelli came from the kitchen, the baby on her shoulder. "Wow, you're here early. Having withdrawal?" She gave him a knowing smile.

With a laugh, he reached out for Abigail. "Yeah, I guess so." Holding her and breathing in her baby smell reassured him she was okay. "Actually, I have some work I need to do in my office. Can you stay?"

"Sure. I have until four o'clock."

He gave the infant a quick kiss on her soft head and passed her back to the babysitter. Time to try to accomplish something for the day.

He couldn't spend every day working from home. He had to find child care he could trust that would allow him to get back out to job sites.

The problem was, he couldn't imagine trusting anyone but Violet.

Violet spread her grandmother's quilt on her back lawn under a large live oak, its graceful branches stretched out as if for the sole purpose of sheltering those resting below. She'd inherited the quilt from her grandfather and appreciated the chance to use it.

The day had been sunny, breezy and a bit less humid than usual. The shade would make a meal outside tolerable.

Trying not to get too excited about the picnic, she set out the hamper she'd packed with food after Jake had accepted her invitation to dinner.

Then she hurried inside for the jug of iced tea. When she returned, she found him standing at the edge of the quilt with Abigail in his arms, the bouncy seat in his other hand and a smile on his face.

"Oh, hey. Glad you made it."

"Thanks for inviting us."

"It's the least I can do after you so kindly brought lunch to the office today." Once Jake had secured Abigail in her bouncy seat, Violet sat down to greet her. She tickled Abigail's feet and spoke to her.

"That would make a great shot." Holding up his phone, Jake took a photo. "I'll email it to Remy through the shelter address. I've already sent her some photos, hoping she'll realize she misses Abigail and want to come back."

"Have you heard from her?"

He didn't need to answer. Disappointment etched itself into his face. "No response yet. And that's assuming the director of the center forwarded the email to Remy."

"Ms. Phillips could be sending through only the ones that she feels are helpful."

"Yeah. And she may consider photos of the baby Remy decided to give up as risky to Remy's well-being."

Violet rubbed Abigail's downy hair. "How could anyone consider this precious girl a threat?"

When Violet looked up, she found Jake staring at her, biting his lip, his blue eyes serious. Her heart stuttered as a sudden breeze blew her hair into her eyes.

She didn't break eye contact, just swiped the strands away. "What's wrong?"

"While I was at your office today, you had a phone call from your mother."

Her blood ran cold, her desire to spend time with Jake vaporizing in an instant. "Sounds as if you were being nosy."

"Maybe. So you want to tell me what's going on with the rift between you and your family? They obviously want to get in touch with you."

"Yes. But we don't see eye to eye on…well, on anything. I don't have the energy to deal with that right now."

"So you're not just being too proud to apologize and work through your problems?"

Admittedly, she was harboring anger. But was she being proud? She'd never thought of that possibility before. Of course, *she* didn't owe *them* the apology. "No, my reticence to return their calls has nothing to do with my being proud. So…how did your day go?"

His eyes narrowed. "I'd like to think after all I shared about my family, you could talk to me."

"I'm more interested in the present. I'd love to know how Kelli worked out."

The glint in his eyes said he wanted to detour back to the original topic. But he didn't push.

"Today was tough," he said, rubbing a finger over Abigail's arm.

"What happened?"

"I got Kelli set up, made sure she could handle Abigail. I went to the job site, but—don't laugh—I thought I heard a baby crying. Thought Kelli was outside with the baby."

A laugh escaped.

"Hey, I told you not to laugh," he said with a grin. "I couldn't handle leaving Abigail with the girl. I left early to work from home."

As selfish as it seemed, she couldn't help the little thrill that shot to her stomach. "I see. Why'd you doubt her capability?"

"She had experience with a six-month-old but not with a baby Abigail's age." He shook his head. "Honestly, she probably would have done fine."

A bird chirped in the tree above them. The warm breeze rippled her hair. The sounds and movement soothed while chaos twisted her insides.

When she looked from the baby into Jake's blue eyes, she found he'd somehow leaned closer to her. They were nearly meeting in the middle over the bouncy seat.

"So why the worry?" she asked. "You've left her with me before."

"Exactly."

The air squeezed out of her lungs, leaving her speechless as she searched his face.

Skimming his finger across Violet's temple, Jake brushed a hair off her cheek. "I've never felt a moment's hesitation leaving Abigail with you."

"Probably because I'm a pediatrician."

"In the beginning, maybe. But it's more than that now."

Her heart did a slow thump-thump, but the longer he looked into her eyes, the more it sped up, like a train chugging along, pulling away from the station.

Whoa. She couldn't let *that* train pull away from the station.

"You know, it's scary," he said. "My little gal here has stolen a piece of my heart."

As their gazes locked, she could almost imagine his look hinted that she, too, had stolen a piece of his heart.

Shaking off the silly thought, she dragged her attention to the baby. "I imagine she has. I think she's stolen a little of mine, as well."

"Makes it tough to leave Abby with just anyone."

So Violet wasn't just anyone, huh? A new thrill surged through her, followed quickly by a dash of reality. She had no business letting this man's words thrill her. "So you've started calling her Abby?"

"It just came out. What do you think?"

"Abby…" Closing her eyes, Violet tried to picture her as a toddler, a teen, even an adult. "I can see her as an Abby. I like it."

He glanced down. "Yeah, I do, too. I wonder if Remy will mind?"

"I think at this point the decision is yours."

"That's pretty sobering."

"I'm afraid the more time that goes by, the less likely it is she'll return. It's already been nearly two weeks."

He tensed, straightened, withdrawing from her space back to his side of the blanket. "I still need time. As you know, I've made progress finding Remy."

He'd made more progress than she ever thought he'd make. "You have. Other than emailing photos, do you have other plans?"

"I thought about hiring a PI, but I don't want to go to that extreme if she doesn't want to be found. And if Remy doesn't want her baby girl enough to come back…Abby doesn't deserve a mom who doesn't want her."

The comment stung. Had her son ever wondered if she'd wanted him? Or, worse, thought she hadn't wanted him?

Violet hurt for Abby. Hurt for Jake. Even hurt for Remy. What a mess of a situation. "I agree."

He took Abby out of her seat and settled her in his arm. "I think she could be happy with me. If I could work out reliable, full-time child care."

She sucked in a breath. He might seriously consider adopting?

What would it be like if Jake had permanent, legal custody of the baby, and Violet spent more time with the two of them? Could they be their own little ragtag group of three?

Jake's phone buzzed. "It's Uncle Paul. Do you mind?"

"No, go ahead."

He swiped the screen to answer. "Hey. Any word on Remy?"

Violet could hear his uncle's deep voice over the line, could even make out an occasional word. While Jake filled in Paul on the domestic violence shelter lead, she tried to busy herself pulling out plates and cups for their picnic.

"I'll send you the director's email address," Jake said. "Let me know if she's more willing to talk to you."

Removing the cover from the chicken salad, Violet gave Jake a smile. He nodded and gave her a thumbs-up.

"The baby's doing well," he said, apparently in answer to a question from his uncle.

The conversation continued, back and forth, Jake telling of his quest to find a babysitter so he could work followed by his uncle's undecipherable words.

"Abby has really taken up with Violet, and I've leaned on her heavily for support."

Silence. Dead silence on the other end of the phone.

Jake's smile tensed, and he glanced away. "She's been a huge help. In fact, we're at her house, about to eat dinner."

More silence.

"I need to get more ice," she whispered with a smile firmly in place, trying to act as if she didn't know of the awful, disapproving void on the line.

Inside the house, she pressed her burning cheek against the cool refrigerator.

She hated when anyone thought badly of her, even if only someone with whom she'd made a business transaction.

Worse, though, was the fact Paul was Jake's family. And for some reason it mattered to her what his family thought.

The back door opened. Violet jerked into motion. Couldn't let him find her upset.

"Need any help?" Jake asked.

She stuck her head inside the cabinet under the counter. "Just looking for the ice bucket. I think all the ice in the tea melted."

"I'm sorry to be rude, answering the phone like that."

"No problem." Her words echoed in the space around the pots and pans. She pressed cool hands to her cheeks, stalling to gain composure.

"Uncle Paul hasn't found any new information, either. He's going to contact the shelter himself."

"That's a good idea." She grabbed the ice bucket. Without a glance in Jake's direction, she stood and headed to the freezer, where she proceeded to fill the bucket.

"My uncle was a little surprised we're getting along so well."

Her hand stilled. Surprise was probably putting it nicely. She finally faced Jake, who stood stiff, uncomfortable, with a sleeping Abigail in his arms.

Might as well bring the awkwardness out in the open. "So Paul thinks you're consorting with the enemy, huh?"

A flash of guilt made him look away. "He didn't realize you'd taken care of Abby outside of the office."

She busied herself putting the lid on the ice, wiping the counter with a dish towel, refolding the cloth. "I guess socializing with your child's doctor isn't the norm."

He laid his hand on her arm, his warm, calloused fingers sending a surge of longing straight to her heart.

"I hope my aunt and uncle will come visit. I'd like for them to get to know you the way I have."

She sure hadn't heard him defending her or asking them to come for that visit. Her heart ached, making it difficult to face him. But she'd never been a coward.

Well…not in several years anyway.

She turned and lifted the corners of her mouth. "I'd like to get to know them."

He leaned against the counter, Abby in one arm sucking a pacifier. "I'm sorry I gave you a hard time when you moved here."

His earnest expression tugged at her, pulling her his direction. Or was it actually his warm hand that was pulling her?

"I understand," she said. "I hope you see that I'm not the person you thought I was."

"Yeah, I'm seeing that more each day. I'd like to try to make amends."

When Violet realized he was staring at her lips, her heart lurched. Could he truly be thinking…?

Slowly, he bent toward her…

His phone buzzed. He jerked upright.

She wanted to groan in frustration but, instead, huffed out a breath she hadn't realized she'd been holding. "Your uncle?"

"I'm not answering it again."

"What if it's important?" she stammered as he scooted closer. Close enough that she knew, this time, he'd actually reeled her toward him while inching his way along the counter toward her.

His phone buzzed again, rattling the cabinet where his hip rested.

He sighed and yanked the phone out of his pocket to look at the screen. "It's Simone."

The name ripped Violet out of her hazy, near-kiss fantasy world. "Take it if you need to."

"No, I'll call her back later."

Maybe he could brush off the phone call, but Violet couldn't. Grasping the ice bucket tightly to her chest, she pulled out of his grasp and headed out the back door. "Time to eat."

Now that she'd started praying again, she wondered if maybe God was trying to tell her something through the near miss.

She didn't need to be getting cozy with Jake West—a man who had women falling all over him and whose family couldn't stand Violet.

A man who knew nothing about her or her past.

Getting close to him was a sure recipe for failure and heartache. Neither of which she could afford. No, she would be much happier if she'd remain focused on her career. The one constant in her life. The one place she had at least some semblance of control.

"Jake, this is Camilla Crenshaw, Violet's mother."

Jake stopped dead in his tracks on the way to put Abby to bed for the night. "What can I do for you?"

"I've been trying to get in touch with my

daughter, and, well…this is a tad embarrassing to admit. She hasn't returned my calls. So I thought I would try to get in contact with her through friends." The woman's voice was deep, cultured. He pictured her standing in a formal living room—eight-inch crown molding, gilded mirrors, custom built-ins—wearing designer clothes and a strand of pearls big enough to choke a horse.

"How did you get my name?"

"Since Appleton is such a small town, I decided to begin by calling local businesses. I had success on my first attempt—the local clothing boutique. The owner, Chloe O'Malley, gave me your name as a close friend of Violet's."

Wow. "Mrs. Crenshaw, I was actually at Violet's office when you called the other day. Couldn't help but hear the receptionist taking the message."

"I've called several times. I'd hoped once Violet started working in that new little town she would have a change of heart."

"I'm not sure where I come in."

"Well, my husband and I would appreciate it if you could speak with Violet, encourage her to return our calls."

"Ma'am, I'd love to see your family reunited. I've encouraged Violet to initiate contact. But since you called me, I'd like to know your intentions."

She hesitated. Was she taken aback by his bluntness?

"I understand your worry." She sighed. "You're being a good friend to our daughter. Let me assure you, we only want the chance to apologize to Violet for not considering her feelings in the past. We've sometimes regretted… that decision."

Did she assume he knew what started the family problems? Jake wished he did so he'd understand Violet better. According to Violet, it had to do with not seeing eye to eye. "Mrs. Crenshaw, Violet hasn't told me what happened with your family. But I'll share your message with her. And I'll make sure she knows why you've been trying to reach her."

"Thank you, Jake. I appreciate this more than you'll ever know. We owe you a favor."

"No favor owed. I'm not doing this for y'all. I'm doing it for Violet."

A laugh similar to Violet's rang across the line. "I like you, Jake West. I'm glad you care enough for Violet to be so direct. My husband and I most certainly do owe you a debt of gratitude."

"I happen to think family is…well, it's everything. I hope Violet will be in touch."

As he hung up, Jake questioned his motive for getting involved. Was he doing this purely because he wanted to see Violet reunited with her family? Or was it deeper than that, maybe the fact he was growing to care for her and wanted her to trust him with her problems?

Who was he kidding? Of course he cared for her. He'd nearly kissed her earlier. Had nearly kissed a woman he barely knew. Yet, after all they'd been through together with Abigail, he felt close to her, as if he knew her at least in part.

But the secrecy with her family issues... She wouldn't open up at all about that. And it apparently had something to do with decisions her parents made that she didn't agree with.

Could it be career related? Had they discouraged her from going to medical school, maybe hadn't had enough faith in her? That could sure cause hurt feelings.

A text message buzzed his phone. From Simone, offering to babysit. He'd forgotten to call her back.

Funny how quickly he'd gotten over their breakup. She'd seemed to recover just as easily and had dated several men in the past year. There shouldn't be any awkwardness if he decided to take her up on her offer.

Why not do it? Though Violet had teased him about Simone, he figured it couldn't hurt to hire her for one week while she was off work.

He texted her back, asking if she could come the next morning. Maybe he'd be at ease leaving Abby with someone more mature.

Then again, maybe not. Because like it or not, whenever he thought of Abby, he immediately put Violet in the picture, as well.

Of course, once she found out her parents had contacted him and he'd agreed to talk to her, she might not forgive him for meddling.

He needed to figure out how to tell her. There was a delicate balance between helping and overstepping.

But her parents wanted to apologize. Weren't apologies always a good thing?

Chapter Eight

Abby's wails filtered through Violet's open screen door, tugging her attention from her computer, making it impossible to concentrate.

She really shouldn't get involved. She had a morning free of appointments, a perfect morning to work at home putting together the training materials for the parenting class she'd be teaching in the fall. She had three glorious hours to catch up on banking and paying bills for the office.

And had absolutely no business stepping into Jake's life if he wanted Simone as a babysitter. But the pitiful child had been crying nonstop for twenty minutes as Simone walked around the backyard. Had the woman even checked Abby's diaper?

Snapping her laptop shut, she popped up out of the kitchen chair, pushed open the back door and marched across the yard toward Jake's house.

She can't just let my baby cry like that.

Violet halted midstep. My baby? *My* baby?

Icy fear settled in her chest as she headed into new territory. Dangerous territory. She'd get in trouble thinking of Abby that way. Remy could return, yanking Abby away as Violet's son had been taken away. Leaving her bereft and broken.

Violet needed to be more careful.

Yet she couldn't let the poor little thing cry until she was hoarse.

Violet approached Jake's patio, where Simone paced trying to console Abby. "Can I help?"

Though she was tense and her expression bordered on panic, Simone was beautiful, exotic with her expertly made-up black eyes and dark wavy hair that cascaded down her back. "Gladly."

When Violet took Abby in her arms, it was as if the baby had taken some sort of chill pill. Her cries hiccuped to a stop. The girl's eyes opened and she studied Violet, as if she recognized her and welcomed being held by her. Almost as if she'd been returned to her own mother.

Love for Abby nearly smothered Violet, making it hard to draw in a full breath. Surely one heart couldn't contain so much love. She brushed Abby's tears away and talked gently to the girl. "You're okay, sweet thing."

"Unbelievable," Simone said. "I think she hates me."

"No, she has bouts of crying sometimes."

Simone wilted into a lounge chair as if exhausted. "How am I ever going to get Jake back if his baby hates me?"

Violet froze. Took a shallow breath.

What had she expected, though? From observing the familiarity between them, she'd suspected Jake and Simone had dated in the past. It made sense that they could get back together, especially now that he needed Simone's help.

But he said he liked having me care for Abby. He acted like he was going to kiss me.

What was wrong with her? First she'd thought of Abby as *my baby*. Now she'd dared think of Jake as her man?

"Here," Violet said. "Take Abby, and I'll show you how she likes to be held."

She wrapped the light summer blanket more tightly around the baby, then set her in the crook of Simone's arm.

"She likes to be swaddled when she's crying. And she likes to be able to look into your face, not be pressed to your chest unless she's snugly in her cloth carrier."

"Oh, okay. I'll see how that works." She bounced a little and smiled at Abby.

The girl's brow scrunched a bit, but she didn't cry.

"That seems to have worked," Simone said, her face lighting with relief. "Thanks."

"I'm glad to help."

"You know, I ruined my chances with Jake before, talking about marriage even though we'd both declared from the beginning that we didn't want anything serious. Kind of freaked him out. But I think Abigail here has changed that. I think he could be ready to settle down."

Jake *had* settled into a routine with the baby and had grown attached. But that didn't mean he was ready to settle into a relationship with a woman. For all Violet knew, he still didn't want anything serious.

Violet certainly didn't need to fall for someone who might avoid commitment. She'd already gone that route with a disastrous end.

The sound of a vehicle pulling up somewhere out front sent her heart racing. It sounded like a large engine, probably Jake's truck. With all the crazy, possessive feelings she'd had that morning, she didn't need to be around him. Time to escape.

"Gotta get back to work." It appeared Abby wasn't going to cry again, so she darted toward home.

"Thanks again," Simone called, probably confused as to why Violet took off so quickly.

She forced herself to politely pause and turn to reply. "You're welcome."

"You know, if Jake gives me another chance at loving him, I'll have you to thank."

The thought of helping Jake reunite with Simone made her cringe, even as she gave a friendly wave goodbye.

Grateful to get away before Jake discovered her, Violet dropped into her chair at the kitchen table. As she opened her computer, she heard Jake greet Simone. Unable to focus on her work, Violet held her head in her hands.

She wanted Jake…but shouldn't. She loved Abby…but shouldn't. She wanted to build a family together… "But I shouldn't, I really shouldn't."

She'd gotten herself into a real mess.

"Violet?" Jake stood outside her screen door ready to knock.

Her face heated. Had he heard her talking to herself? "Come on in."

His smile wreaked havoc on her insides, making them flutter and dance and compress her lungs so she could hardly breathe.

He stood there in jeans and a button-up work shirt, wiping his dusty boots on her doormat. Then he stepped inside. "Hey."

"Hey," she replied, the only coherent thing she could manage at the moment. Why did he have to look and smell so good after he'd spent the morning working?

"I really appreciate you helping Simone. She told me you'd stopped Abby's crying."

"I just showed her how she likes to be held."

"Funny how we both know Abby's likes and dislikes." He slipped his hands in his pockets. "I'm feeling more like a parent every day."

He acted more like one, too. So gentle and protective. "You're really good with her."

He gestured to the chair beside her at the end of the rectangular oak table.

She nodded. "Have a seat."

"I have to admit, the more time that passes, the more I have the crazy urge to quit looking for Remy and adopt Abby."

Torn, Violet didn't know what to say. The wishful dreamer in her would love for him to do just that. But the realist thought he needed to give Remy every chance to step up.

"I can understand that. What do you think you'll do?"

He sighed and ran a hand through his hair. "Still deciding. I'd really like to talk to Remy before I take any legal action." He spotted her open computer. "Working at home today?"

Scrunching her brow, she said, "Yeah, my only appointment this morning canceled." Which didn't bode well for staying in the black this month.

He looked distressed by that fact. "I'm sure business will pick up soon." He started to say something, then stopped. "I should let you get back to whatever you were doing. Thanks again for coming to Abby's rescue."

"Glad to help."

His grateful expression dimmed, turned serious. "Actually, if you have a minute, I need to talk to you. And I hope you'll understand that I'm only trying to help."

A sense of foreboding made her stomach muscles tighten. "Help with what?"

"Your mother called, and I spoke with her."

Ice cold ran through her veins. Had her mother told him anything? Did he know she'd had a baby?

"Look, I can tell you're not happy, but—"

"You had no right. My relationship with my parents is none of your business."

"Well, I kind of think it is sort of my business." Irritation sparked in his eyes.

"Why on earth would you think that?"

"Because I care about you."

Cared *about* her. Not cared *for* her. There was a huge difference. "I'm not buying that excuse."

He plunked back in his chair, looking wounded. "I spoke with her because I knew she'd been trying to contact you. I wanted to find out why, to make sure you wouldn't be hurt."

How could he assure that? Her parents had hurt her over and over and weren't likely to change. She swiped her suddenly damp palms on her shorts, then stood. "I think you should leave."

"Your mother said they only want the chance to apologize because they regret their decision."

A wave of dizziness swept over Violet, forcing her to grip the table edge. *Now* they regretted the decision?

She needed to get Jake out of her house to process what he'd told her. "Please leave." *Does he know? Surely not from the way he's looking at me with concern. Because he'll loathe me once he finds out the truth.*

He moved toward the door. "I hope you'll agree to meet with them, that you'll give them a chance for reconciliation."

If he knew what happened, he wouldn't expect her to be so forgiving. "I request you to stay out of my personal business in the future."

As if a wall had slid in place, the warmth in his eyes cooled. "Fine."

She'd hurt him. Angered him, even. But he was an honorable man shouldering the responsibility of a child who wasn't his, making sacrifices, trying his best to parent Abby and do the right thing. If he kept digging around in her past, talking to her parents, he'd find out the truth and would realize she'd been weak and selfish.

When her parents had refused to help her raise her son and pushed her to give him up for adoption, she'd let fear—and her dream of becoming a big-shot surgeon—sway her decision. Sure, Jake might admire her for helping with

Abby. But what would he think of her when he discovered that she hadn't done the same for her own child?

As soon as Simone arrived Wednesday morning to babysit, Jake put her in charge of feeding Abby, then he stepped out the back door into the drizzling rain.

They'd have a muddy day at the work site.

He sprinted toward Violet's house, hoping to catch her before she left for work. To apologize. Last night, the more he'd thought about the situation, the more he realized he should have taken Camilla Crenshaw's number, said he would call her back, then checked with Violet.

Knocking on the back door, he huddled under the overhang to try to stay dry. She didn't answer, so he ran around to the front door and rang the bell.

The door opened immediately. "Oh. Jake." She stood in her work clothes with her purse on her shoulder, keys in hand. "I was just leaving."

"Do you have a second?"

Her eyes narrowed, and he felt sure she didn't want to give him a moment of her time.

"I came to apologize."

She stood, arms crossed in front of her. "I'm glad you realize the need."

"I shouldn't have spoken to your mother without checking with you first."

"No, you shouldn't have."

Her certainty sparked a flash of irritation. "I still think it needed to be done, though. I was only protecting you, looking out for your best interests."

"I don't need your protection."

The comment hurt. He'd thought they'd shared something…some connection. More than friendship. "So I can need you, but you can't need me, huh?"

Surprise widened her eyes. "You need me?"

All the closeness he'd felt fizzled. Why did she have to look so shocked? Hadn't she felt the same thing?

Apparently not.

He sure wasn't going to open up and spill his guts if she wasn't feeling it, too. "I'll let you get to work."

"No, tell me what you mean by needing me."

"I need your…friendship. Your help with Abby."

The look of disappointment on her face gave him pause.

"You know I'm happy to help anytime," she said, stern and efficient. "Who's lined up to babysit today?"

He fought a frustrated sigh. They were back to business as usual. "Simone's there now. I'm still working on finding someone to do mornings. Kelli is coming again this afternoon."

"And you'll manage to stay away for more than five minutes?" she said in all seriousness. Yet maybe…yes, she had a teasing glint in her eyes.

He laughed. "I have to. I've got a meeting late this afternoon."

She pulled her phone out of her purse and scrolled to look at something. "I can take a little time to drop by, maybe go over some basics with Kelli—first aid, that kind of thing. It'll give me peace of mind, as well."

He wanted to wrap her in his arms and ask how she could care so much about Abby yet not feel anything for him.

"Thanks, Violet. I'd really appreciate you doing that."

Locking her phone, she stuffed it back in her bag. "I'll be there around one o'clock."

"I should let you go," he said. "Again, I'm sorry for upsetting you by speaking with your mother. I hope you'll forgive me."

A hint of a smile made her lips twitch. "So you're not sorry for interfering, just sorry that you upset me?"

He grinned. "Pretty much."

She poked a finger at his chest. "Isn't that like apologizing for getting caught?" Her sparkling eyes locked with his, humor lighting her face as she leaned toward him. Probably without realizing it.

"I guess it is."

Rain poured outside, pounding the roof, making the entryway of her home feel isolated, intimate. Thunder sounded in the distance, mimicking how his world had just shifted.

He needed to touch Violet when she looked at him like that, almost flirty, as if she truly liked him. He stepped into her space. Though she held her purse like a defensive shield, he reached out and brushed a stray piece of hair back from her forehead. "But I do feel bad that my actions upset you—even if I'd do it all over again trying to protect you, to maybe help you heal."

Her head tilted. "So you think my mother just wants to apologize?"

"Sounded like it to me."

She pulled in a deep breath, then let it out slowly. "Then I'll *consider* calling them."

He smirked. "You're as good at playing with words as I am."

"Hey, I learned from a master, my mother, a society belle with a gilded tongue."

"She sounded genuine on the phone."

"Don't let her suck you in."

Moving closer, he slid the purse off her shoulder and set it on the entry table. Then he took her warm, small hand and threaded his fingers through hers, the gesture so intimate he wasn't sure she'd tolerate it.

Again, her big hazel eyes widened. Thankfully, she didn't move away.

"Violet, have you ever considered that maybe your mother has changed? That maybe she and your father love you and want to reestablish a relationship?"

"I'll consider the possibility. That's as far as I can go at the moment."

He nodded. "Okay, I won't push." He brushed his thumb over her thumb. "You haven't said you forgive me."

Her shoulders relaxed. Leaning closer, she gazed at him, eyes playful, vibrant. "I'll consider it."

With a chuckle, he lifted her chin. He wanted to kiss her. Badly. But he feared it was too soon. She didn't even trust him enough to share more than superficial things about her parents.

Instead, he smoothed his finger across her soft cheek. Then he took hold of her other hand so that they faced each other, fingers locked. "I won't let you go until you say you forgive me."

"Okay, okay. I forgive you," she said with a laugh.

"Good. Now, please don't forget to drop by and check out Kelli's babysitting abilities so I can rest easy."

"You can count on me."

"Thanks." He begrudgingly let go of her hands. "We'll talk later."

Regret gnawed at him as he returned home. She was able to do him a favor because business was slow. A few unkind words here and there had hurt her practice. Venting to friends of his aunt and uncle had probably caused the spread of rumors.

If Violet wouldn't let him help with her parents, then maybe he could help with her practice.

He'd make a few phone calls. Would quietly get word out that Violet Crenshaw was a great doctor and a much better person than he'd thought before meeting her. Violet was a good woman, generous, dedicated, fun. A woman he was growing to care deeply about.

And that was the honest truth. No wordplay needed.

"So what's up with you and Jake?"

Startled by Hillary's question, Violet froze with her hand on the menu. "Not a thing. I've just been wearing my doctor's hat, helping him with Abby. I even trained one of his babysitters on Wednesday."

The receptionist, wearing brightly patterned, kid-friendly scrubs that she'd worked in that day, gave a snort. "Uh-huh."

At her doubtful tone, Violet jerked her gaze to the woman. However, Hillary focused on running her finger down the plastic-coated menu of Edna's Diner.

Edna darted their way. "What're y'all having, ladies? I've got some nice fried catfish for my Friday night special. And also smothered chicken," she drawled, the *smother* sounding like *smuthuh*, just as Violet's mother always said it.

The quick memory jabbed at her heart—made tender by Jake's revelation the other day.

"I'll have the meatloaf. My regular," Hillary said with a smile as she handed over her menu.

"And I'll try the smothered chicken."

Edna rushed away to place their order.

Time to get to the point of their meeting. "Hillary, I need your advice."

The woman, who'd worked for Paul and Edith for more than ten years, leaned her arms on the table and focused on Violet, all teasing gone. "Gladly."

"I know we've had a good week—or at least a good *end* of the week—patient-wise."

"Yeah. Felt busier than usual."

"But I'm still concerned. I'm considering closing one day a week to help save on utilities and payroll."

Hillary hesitated but didn't look surprised. "That could be smart. But it could also be inconvenient for patients, so we might lose more."

She sighed. "That's why I wanted to run the idea by you, since you have so much experience in a medical office. And because you'd lose a day's pay."

"Have you done anything else to get your name out there?"

Violet brightened, glad she had good news on that front. "Actually, I have. I've volunteered to teach the parenting class at the hospital. I'm going to speak to the elementary school PTO. And I've got a call in to the director of the hospital to offer my services doing rounds in the newborn nursery."

"Sounds like you'll make a lot of connections. Maybe wait a little longer before you cut back. I don't mind giving up a day a week if it would help. You can answer the phones and check patients in."

"Seriously? You'd be willing to do that?"

"Look, I'm sure it'll be temporary. Trust me, business will pick up once you put yourself out in the community. In fact, I overheard two women talking in line at the bank at lunchtime today."

Violet's stomach sank. She groaned.

Hillary put her hand on Violet's arm. "No, it was good. One told the other she'd been hearing good things from her contractor. Said she had already made an appointment for her children for a well visit. The other said she was tired of driving so far to see their pediatrician and would do the same."

Heaving a sigh of relief, Violet leaned back in her chair. "Maybe we're going to make it."

With a reassuring squeeze, Hillary gave a firm nod. "Oh, I know we will."

Violet covered Hillary's hand. "Thank you. You've been a huge help—as usual."

"Seems you've been a huge help to Jake."

At the abrupt change of subject, Violet shook her head, smiling. "I told you, Abby's my patient."

Hillary held her gaze, searching. Desperately afraid Hillary would see how much she already cared about Jake, Violet glanced away.

"Violet, honey, there's nothing to be ashamed about if you're feeling more. Jake's a good guy."

With her face burning, Violet fiddled with the sugar and pink sweetener packets. "I know he is."

With a sympathetic expression, Hillary leaned closer. "He had a rough childhood, you know. But he never let losing his parents get him down. He took care of Remy like she was his own sister. Tried his best to keep her out of trouble. I'm not a bit surprised he's stepped up to care for Abby."

Exactly as Violet had discovered. Jake was an honorable man. A man who wanted to do the right thing. Who even wanted to help reunite her family.

But would he commit to Violet as he'd committed to Abby? More than anything, she wanted to trust him. But could she really after what Simone had said about him not wanting to marry?

"He's a handsome man with a thriving business," Hillary added, a sly smile tilting one corner of her mouth. "A real catch. You'd be crazy not to be interested in dating him."

Violet couldn't help but laugh at Hillary's sales pitch. "Oh, we don't have anything romantic going on."

"Uh-huh," she said, just as she'd said earlier.

Hillary's cell phone buzzed. She pulled it out of her purse and checked the screen. "Excuse me for a minute. I need to take this." She slipped out of the booth and glanced back over her shoulder. "Just know that you can't go wrong with Jake West."

Nothing romantic going on? What about in her entry hall the other day? Jake had entwined his fingers with hers, his touch tripping her pulse. When he'd brushed his fingers across her face, her heart had soared, and she'd thought he might pull her close. Then he'd tilted her chin upward, his gaze on her lips as if he wanted to kiss her, and she'd held her breath in anticipation, wanting him to. Wanting it so badly she nearly closed the space between them herself.

Violet realized she was once again holding her breath and huffed the air out. Fanned herself with her napkin. Honestly, she needed to get hold of her vacillating emotions.

He *hadn't* kissed her, though. Even though she'd looked up at him as if starving for his kiss. He'd had every opportunity to claim her lips with his. But instead, he'd simply pushed for forgiveness.

Why? He'd sure seemed to *want* to kiss her. Something was holding him back. Maybe a fear of commitment? The man had suffered great loss in his childhood, had struggled to please his aunt and uncle. And now, with getting attached to Abby while wondering whether or not Remy would return, he risked major heartbreak again.

Maybe he simply didn't have room for Violet in his life.

If she knew what was good for her, she'd ignore Hillary and forget silly notions of romance.

Chapter Nine

Jake picked up Abby from where she had spent some time lying on a blanket on her stomach. He nuzzled her neck and brought her sweet hand to his mouth to kiss it.

Tiny fingernails scratched the corner of his mouth. "Ouch, baby girl. Your nails need to be cut." And no one was around to help.

Maybe the task would be easier after a bath, when her nails would be softer.

"Come on, sweet thing." Carrying her in the crook of his arm, he went to the bathroom in search of the baby toiletry kit that included clippers and scissors.

He located both and inspected the miniature tools. How could something so small feel so intimidating? Give him a chainsaw any day.

Imagining snipping the nearly microscopic nails growing close to Abby's delicate skin made him break out in a cold sweat. No way would he attempt something that could draw blood.

He pulled out his phone. Even though it was eight o'clock on a Friday night, he hit Call on Violet's name.

On the third ring, she picked up. "Hey."

"I need help."

"What's wrong?" she asked with a note of panic in her voice.

"Itsy-bitsy razor-sharp baby fingernails. Gigantic nail clippers."

She laughed. "They make infant nail clippers, you know."

"Those are the ones I'm talking about. How soon can you come?"

Silence.

"I'm sorry. Do you have plans?"

"No plans. I'll be right over."

"We'll be in the bathroom doing the bath routine. Come on in the back door."

Jake gathered everything he needed, then filled the baby tub and placed it on the counter. He slipped Abby in the warm water and began washing her. What had been a dreaded chore two weeks ago had begun to feel like a bonding ritual. Maybe because she didn't scream through it anymore.

Abby kicked her feet a little, almost as if she were enjoying bath time now.

"You two look like you're having fun." Violet

stood in the doorway wearing running shorts and an old T-shirt. The duo seemed to be her go-to nonwork outfit. That and her flip-flops.

"I love seeing you in your regular clothes."

"My mother never abided lounging clothes. So now I wear them whenever I get the chance."

Trying to imagine the serious doctor bucking authority, he grinned. "Ever the rebel, huh?"

"So where are the clippers?" she asked, avoiding talking about her past.

"In that zippered bag."

Violet dug inside and pulled them out. "Here, let's get those vicious nails off."

She leaned around him while he finished rinsing Abby's legs. Pressed up against his side, she lifted Abby's tiny hands and carefully, yet confidently, snipped off the tips of the fingernails with the clippers.

He breathed in the scent of Violet's shampoo, relished the feel of her warmth against his shoulder. "Wow. You're a pro. I would have taken forever and would have been terrified of hurting her."

She lifted his hand, then held up the tiny clippers beside his fingers. "No contest. And I don't think those sausage fingers will fit in the scissors, either."

Having her close made his chest feel tight. "Guess I'll just have to call you to come over for each nail trim."

"Anytime." She brushed soap bubbles off Abby's cheek. "How's my girl doing today?"

"She had a good day with Kelli." He grabbed a plastic cup and filled it with fresh water. "Want to help me wash her hair? She doesn't usually cooperate as well on this part."

"Dry her off and wrap her up. I'll show you an easier way to do it."

He did as told. Then Violet took Abby from him, holding the bundled up baby along the underside of her left forearm with Abby's head cupped in her palm. She held her over the sink.

As she used her right hand to scoop warm tap water over Abby's hair, he stepped in to see better.

"See, she's totally secure, and the water is nice and warm. Secure and warm equals happy baby." She smiled up at him, and he realized he'd quit watching the demonstration. He was watching the beautiful, gentle pediatrician. The warm, generous woman.

Secure and warm equaled happy man, too.

Slipping his arm around her waist—his contribution to the hair-washing—he pushed Violet's wispy dark hair behind her ear.

"Jake, watch what I'm doing. You'll be able to do this until she gets too big."

Forcing his attention back to Abby, he tried to concentrate.

Scoop water. Lather. Rinse.

Abby lay there totally content, dark hair slicked to her head, blue eyes wide open, looking at them both as if they were this perfect family of three.

"All done." Violet finished rinsing, then pulled up a corner of the bath towel to dry Abby's head.

"I think I can manage trying that next time," he said. "Thanks."

Wrapped in Violet's arms, Abby yawned, and her eyes grew heavy.

Jake rubbed the tightness from his chest. He hated for Violet to leave so soon, and he had a feeling she might like to be involved in more than the bath. "Bottle and bedtime. You want to do the honors?"

She blinked. Nodded.

"How about you get her diapered and dressed while I make the bottle?" he said.

"I'll be happy to."

"I guess you know where everything is. A clean sleeper is on the bed."

While preparing the formula, Jake took his time moving around the kitchen. Slowly, deliberately, he opened the can and poured it in the bottle. Soon, Abby would fall asleep and they'd put her in the bed. Then he would be alone with Violet.

He wanted to kiss her. It was all he'd been thinking about for days.

But he shouldn't.

His aunt and uncle didn't trust her, though they didn't know her as well as he did.

She was secretive and wouldn't open up to him, even after he'd shared about himself.

Plus, she'd made it perfectly clear she was focused on her career.

He was crazy for getting sucked in to the coziness. Especially when Remy could come back tomorrow and shatter the bond the three of them had formed.

"Jake, she's ready and about to fall asleep." Violet stood in the doorway of the kitchen, contentment shining in her beautiful hazel eyes, Abby cradled in her arms.

"Here you go." He held out the bottle to her. "I don't have a nice rocking chair, but Uncle Paul's old lounger in the family room has done the trick."

"Sounds perfect." She smiled as she shifted Abby to one arm, yet her expression was full of longing. Maybe she felt the bond as strongly as he did.

Determination settled fully into his bones. Tonight, if they got to know each other better, if she would open up to him even a little or give any hint that she'd started to trust him…he *would* kiss her.

With her hand trembling, Violet took the bottle from Jake.

Why was she shaking so?

Why, my eye. I'm shaking because he keeps staring at my lips. Because he's standing so close I can see that his blue eyes have a dark blue ring around them that's almost purple.

I'm shaking because after we put Abby to bed, I want to beg him to quit looking at me like I'm a tasty morsel and just kiss me already.

Violet escaped the tension by darting to the living room and settling in the worn leather recliner. Touching the nipple to Abby's lips, she roused the baby.

Jake sat nearby on the dark green tweed couch, arms resting on his knees, watching Abby eat.

Once again, Violet felt as if they were a normal family, taking care of their own child. Warm and cozy herself, Violet relaxed. Sighed.

"You seem happy." Jake reached over and stroked Abby's head.

"I love holding this precious child."

"Me, too. With having child care and getting back to work nearly full-time the last couple of days, Abby and I have finally found a rhythm."

"So Kelli and Simone worked out okay?"

"Yeah. Between the two of them, they had the babysitting covered. I realized I was probably being overly concerned."

"That's normal. Most parents are that way with first children."

He leaned against the back of the couch and scraped a hand across his beard. "I want to adopt her."

Her heart fluttered, like delicate wings battering against stifled hope.

Yet Jake's simple statement was fraught with what-ifs. She had to tread carefully. "Do you think maybe you need to give Remy more time?"

"I've been emailing her daily, sending photos, begging to meet with her. She hasn't responded since that first time through the director."

Abby's eating had slowed, yet she continued sucking on the bottle.

"You're assuming the director of the shelter is passing along your messages," Violet said.

"I confirmed with Ms. Phillips that Remy has received all my messages. If she hasn't contacted me yet, I don't think she will."

"Well, you know her better than anyone else does."

Jake stuck his pinkie finger in Abby's palm, and she gripped it. The sight of a big man hand nestled with a tiny baby hand brought tears to her eyes.

"I can understand wanting to make a clean break from Abby if that's Remy's final decision," he said. "But why won't she meet with just me? Though I've been denying it, my gut says either she's in an abusive situation, or she's on drugs again. If that's the case, I can't keep waiting for her to show up. I have to permanently protect Abby."

"I'm sorry, Jake. The thought of Remy choosing drugs over her baby is unimaginable."

"When addiction takes control, it's excruciating to watch."

Especially when, according to Hillary, he'd been the one protecting her all those years. In the back of her mind, though, she wondered... "So you don't think there's any chance she brought Abby to you because she felt overwhelmed and ill equipped to care for a child?"

"If that were the case, I think she would have missed Abby enough to come back by now."

Violet kissed the baby's forehead, breathing in her powdery baby shampoo scent. "I'd like to give Remy the benefit of the doubt, but whatever the reason, I guess she made her choice."

"Like you made your choice about severing ties with your family?"

The sudden change of topic hit her in the solar plexus, leaving her off balance. Could she keep the conversation out of personal territory? "Yes, I did."

"Why?"

She'd lived her whole adult life without anyone knowing the full truth. Sad to admit, but no one really knew her at all.

Looking into his kind eyes, she wanted to tell

him, to share at least some of her past. She sensed he wouldn't judge her, not harshly anyway.

"My parents let me down when I needed them most. They hurt me terribly."

Abby's mouth had grown slack, and the bottle nipple slipped out. Violet set the uneaten ounce of formula down and placed the baby on her shoulder, patting gently to burp her.

"I'm sorry," Jake said. "Did they fail to support you becoming a physician?"

"Oh, they supported my career aspirations— at the expense of everything else. By the time I left for college, I was so angry I broke off ties. I put myself through college and medical school." With Abby pressed to her chest, she ached for the times she'd missed with her own child. If only she'd been strong enough, selfless enough, to give up her career goals and keep her baby no matter what her parents wanted.

As Abby's eyes closed, Jake stood and held out a hand to Violet.

Her heart pounded as she put her hand in his. He helped her up, then ushered her to Abby's bedroom.

Violet laid the girl in the travel bed. "Looks as if you may need to buy a real crib soon."

"It's on my list to do this weekend." He tucked loose edges of the receiving blanket underneath Abby. "I kind of feel like buying something permanent will make good things happen. And of course, I'm trying to trust God in the situation."

Violet crossed her arms tightly in front of her. "Yeah, I've been trying, too, for the first time in a long time. And not doing too well at it."

The room was small, dimly lit, intimate. His tender smile left her feeling vulnerable.

"I'm glad you're coming to church."

"I'll be there again this Sunday," she said, trying to sound upbeat. Instead, having him so near and looking at her so intently caused her breath to catch and her words to sound airy.

"Do you trust me yet?" he asked.

You can't afford to trust anyone, her brain told her. But at the moment, she didn't want to think. She wanted to stand close to Jake, who smelled so good, whose warmth she craved. "I'm trying to."

"I'm not out to hurt you, you know. I care for you."

Her pulse thrummed in her ears. She cared for him, too. But the words remained locked inside her head, inside her heart. "I think I've seen evidence that you care."

"Oh?"

"We had several new patients the end of this week. Also had new patients making appointments for checkups."

"That's good news." He looked pleased and not one bit surprised she'd changed the subject.

"I imagine I have you to thank for that."

He brushed her hair behind her ear, then smoothed his palm over her jawline. "You've impressed parents with your caring and expertise. They must be talking."

"I have a feeling it's more than that. Thank you." His touch soothed her. Some rare sense of daring made her want to take a risk, so she pressed her cheek against his palm.

In the dark, makeshift nursery, lit only by the small night-light in the corner, he pulled her close. Cupped her cheeks in his warm, rough hands. "I don't know what the future may hold with Abby. But one thing is certain. I want more with you, more than friendship. More than your pediatric expertise. I want…"

"What, Jake? What do you want?" she barely breathed, the words a choked whisper.

"This." His eyes fell closed as he touched his lips to hers.

Her heart whizzed and soared, like fireworks shot to the sky, yet warm, full lips moving over hers kept her rooted to the earth. Her heart lay open, ready to love and be loved. When she touched his face, he intensified the kiss.

"Oh, Violet," he whispered, touching his forehead to hers. "I wanted to do that days ago, but the timing didn't feel right. I'm glad you opened up a little about your family. But I want to know everything about you."

Like a cold north wind seeping in through a window, the comment slowly invaded her fantasy world—the world where she kissed a handsome man who said he cared for her. Could she handle having a relationship? How would he feel once he found out about her past?

Would he think her weak, or worse, selfish?

"I should go," she said, forcing herself away from his touch.

"Yeah, okay. Probably a good idea." A deep laugh rumbled in his chest as he dragged his gaze from her lips.

"Wha— Oh." Her face flushed. He thought she meant to leave because of the sizzling attraction. Although she was actually escaping the truth. Truth that might change his feelings about her.

He wanted to know everything about her. Before she committed to a relationship, she *wanted* him to know everything, *needed* him to know. First, she had to figure out how to tell him. How to explain emotions she still hadn't fully processed, especially now that her parents claimed they regretted their decision about her son.

Maybe the past wasn't so cut and dried. Now that she'd witnessed Jake's love for Abby, she had to acknowledge her son had probably had a better life than she could have offered as a teen without any support.

Despite her parents' motivations, maybe they had ultimately done what was best for everyone.

Maybe God had heard her desperate prayers all along, had taken a painful situation and worked it out for good.

"Um, yeah. I was just leaving." She gave him a timid smile, then turned to walk away.

With a gentle tug on her hand, he reeled her back in. "One for the road, Doc." He planted a quick kiss on her lips, then gave her a smile as he let go. "Thanks for once again coming to my rescue."

"Anytime." With a wave, she headed out.

If she believed God worked everything out for good, then she'd have to trust Him when revealing her past to Jake.

She needed to do it soon.

"Looks like you've been bitten by the love bug," Zeb cracked so loudly that the other men at the work site heard.

Snickers sounded around the corner.

Jake's neck probably glowed as red as Zeb's shiny new truck. He hadn't even intended to mention Violet. He'd started the conversation talking about possibly adopting Abby.

That morning, he'd decided he would email Remy one more time, warning her of his plan to contact an attorney. But telling Zeb about Abby invariably led to talking about Violet.

"What makes you say that?" Jake asked.

"I see it in your eyes when you talk about Doc Crenshaw. That and the big stupid grin on your face."

Clamping his teeth together to wipe away that telltale smile, he clicked Abby's car seat in the base and shut the truck door. She sat happily in her car seat, sucking on a pacifier. Jake climbed in behind the wheel, relieved that she hardly ever cried anymore. No more colic, if that was what had caused her crying jags. She only cried when she was hungry or needed changing. Or sometimes in her car seat.

"Gotta go before Abby starts fretting. Be sure to send me that bid we talked about."

"Will do," Zeb said. "I'm happy for you. I hear Doc Crenshaw is a great gal. A fine doctor."

Glad to hear people were finally seeing Violet for the amazing person she was, he gave a firm nod. "She is. And just between you and me, I plan to ask her out."

Zeb slapped his leg and cackled. "I knew it."

"Don't mention it. She doesn't know yet."

"Oh, don't worry. Wouldn't want to humiliate you if she turns you down." He winked at Jake and headed inside.

Zeb was joking, but he'd hit a raw nerve. Jake was worried about that very thing.

No, he was going to think positively. Hadn't Violet taught him not to give up? After last night, everything felt right between them. Mostly. She hadn't opened up fully, but she'd taken a step, talking about her parents' high expectations, their focus on career.

Of course, she'd left quickly. But then, she had a tendency to do that.

As he pulled out onto the road, he couldn't help but smile. Last night had been perfect. He was glad he'd waited to kiss her. But she still hadn't told him exactly what had happened to tear apart her family. She'd kind of danced around it. Uncertainty niggled at him as he drove home.

When he arrived, he took Abby inside. As he lifted her out of her seat, and she looked him in the eye, a wave of protectiveness nearly brought him to his knees. He loved this little girl as if she were his own.

He would type up an email to Remy. Would give her one last chance to act. Then on Tuesday, he would contact a lawyer to pursue officially adopting Abby.

Jake fed Abby her lunch and then put her down for a nap. He opened a new email and started typing.

Dear Remy,
I hope you've been reading my messages. I'm starting to wonder if you've fallen back into the clutches of addiction. Whatever the reason

you're not replying, I need you to know that I love Abby. She's taken over my heart, and I want to make her a permanent part of my life.

From what you've said, you want me to raise her. If I don't hear from you by Monday evening, I'm consulting an attorney to start legal proceedings for adoption.

I know this is what you said you wanted in the first place, but I've wanted to give you every chance to come home to get your daughter. However, now I need to move to the next step. For Abby's well-being as well as for my peace of mind.

I truly hope you're doing well. I pray for you daily.

Love, Jake

Jake saved the email but didn't send it. He picked up his phone and texted Violet, asking her to come over to read the message. He felt he needed her input, her approval.

Ten minutes later, she walked in his kitchen door.

"Wearing your uniform, I see." He smiled at her Nike shorts and dark green T-shirt.

"You know it."

After an awkward moment, he stepped into her space and wrapped his arms around her waist. "You look good no matter what you're wearing."

She smiled up at him. "I know I don't, but you're sweet for saying it. Where's Abby?"

"Asleep." He leaned down and kissed her cheek. "Mmm, you smell good."

"I took a shower after seeing patients at the office and checking on a baby at the hospital."

He kissed her forehead, her nose and then finally her mouth. It had been way too long since he'd kissed her.

She wrapped her arms around his neck and melted into him, her warm lips pressed to his.

"Lord, take me now, and I'll die a happy man," he whispered against her lips.

She laughed. Inched away. "You're crazy."

"Just thanking God for you." Staring into her eyes that looked extra green today against her green shirt, he brushed the wispy ends of her hair off her forehead. "Now, before I forget the whole reason for asking you to come over…"

He flipped open his computer. "I'd like you to read this before I send it. Give me your honest opinion."

"Okay." Violet settled into the chair and read. And read.

She continued to stare at the screen well beyond a reasonable length of time.

"What's wrong? Is it too strong, not strong enough? Is it—"

"It's perfect." She looked up at him with tears brimming in her eyes. "If there's any chance she still wants Abby, this should spur her to act quickly. If there's no hope of her coming…well, this will reassure her that her baby will be well loved, will have a happy life."

Jake swallowed a knot the size of a two-by-four out of his throat. "Then let's hit the send button."

She moved the cursor, he put his hand over hers and they clicked together.

"Thank you." He pulled her to her feet. "For your support, for making me believe I can do this. And also for allowing me to keep Abby out of the system."

"I hope Remy takes this email to heart."

"Is it wrong of me to hope she doesn't show?"

She sighed, her expression thoughtful. "I think it's normal. But you should be prepared for her to come."

He tightened his arms, hugging her to his chest. "I'm trying to. But in my worst nightmares, she does show up, high on drugs, trying to steal Abby away. If that happens, I'll call the police."

"Being ready is good." Patting her hand over his heart, she smiled. "But don't borrow trouble."

He stepped back. "You're right. Just two more days, and we'll know."

She smiled and touched his face. "Think positively."

"I am. In fact, I'd like to take you out on Friday. To celebrate starting the adoption process."

"Wow. That's certainly thinking positively."

His heart plummeted. She hadn't exactly jumped at the offer. "So, how about it? We'll get a babysitter, maybe go out for a nice dinner. And hey, my birthday's next weekend. You can hardly say no to that."

"Your birthday? I should be the one taking you out."

Lifting her hand to his mouth, he kissed her palm. "So will you go out with me?"

Biting her lip, she glanced away. "I need to check my schedule. Can I let you know tomorrow?"

Check her schedule? Sounded like an excuse to him. "Sure."

She looked up at him, tentative, unsure.

Still holding her hand, he pressed it to his chest, near his heart. "This may sound crazy, but I feel hopeful. When I'm with you and Abby, I feel like I have everything that's been missing in my life." Suddenly uncomfortable for saying the words out loud, he let go of her hand and slid his into his pockets.

Her eyes widened, but she didn't step away.

Might as well go for broke. "It's like I have the family I've always longed for."

"I'm glad…you, uh…have that," she said, the words a struggle to push out.

The sound of Abby shuffling in her bed filtered through the baby monitor. Then she whimpered.

Violet let out a puff of air, no doubt relieved. "I should leave. I need to run some errands."

"Oh, okay. Guess I'll see you at church tomorrow."

"Yep. See you then." She smiled and headed out the back door.

He'd scared her off by asking her out. Or, more likely, by mentioning the family thing.

Surely she wanted that bond, that family connection, as much as he did. He'd have to be patient and give her time to accept the fact they needed each other.

Chapter Ten

I have a potential date on Friday.

For about the hundredth time since yesterday, a thrill shot through Violet when she thought of Jake asking her out.

What on earth was she going to do?

She glanced at him sitting in the pew on the other side of Abby's carrier, not two feet away. He was so handsome it made her insides dance all over the place every time she looked at him. But more than that, he was strong, dependable, loyal.

Loyalty was huge. A trait she required a man to have before she would go out with him. Of course, she had already kissed Jake. Why hesitate to make a relationship official with a date?

Regardless, she should do something nice to celebrate his birthday.

As they stood for the last hymn, Violet decided she would grab Chloe after the service to get suggestions for a possible gift. When the music ended, the pastor dismissed them.

She looked over at Jake. "Nice service."

"Yeah. And a beautiful day outside, too."

Okay, so he was talking about the weather, feeling some of the same awkwardness. She didn't feel so bad.

She rubbed Abby's head. "See you later, sweet girl."

"In a hurry?"

"I need to catch Chloe."

He nodded toward the front of the church. "She's over there with her sister."

"Thanks." Her stomach had been knotted since she awoke. Before the service, Jake had informed her Remy hadn't responded to his email. Could she have contacted him in the past hour?

"Will you check your email again before I go?" she asked.

He gave her an understanding smile and looked relieved she felt the same. "Was about to do that." He pulled his phone out of his pocket, unlocked it and quickly checked messages.

What would Jake do if his cousin wanted Abby?

"No word from Remy."

The tension rushed out in a huff. "I can't stand to think of her coming back and doing that to you, even though I believe Remy deserves a chance." She wished she could ban the possibility. She didn't want to see Jake hurt.

He took her hand and gave it a squeeze. "Thanks. That means the world to me. So… about Friday…" Laughter pulled his attention to the other side of the church. "Oh, looks like Chloe's heading out. You better hurry."

With her face warm, she let go of his hand. "Thanks. I'll talk to you about Friday later." She darted toward her friends. "Chloe, Darcy, wait up!"

They paused in the open door. As Darcy waved, the diamond in her new gorgeous engagement ring caught the sunlight and flashed.

A stab of envy left Violet feeling sucker punched. *Since when do I care about romance and marriage?*

Who was she kidding? She'd started caring the moment she'd realized Jake was not only handsome, but also a good man determined to keep his promise to care for Abby.

"Hi, Violet. What's up?" Chloe asked.

"I just found out Jake's birthday is this coming weekend. Wanted to see what y'all would suggest I do for a gift."

"Got a hot date with the birthday boy?" Chloe teased.

Darcy swatted at her sister's arm. "Give Violet a break."

"It's okay," Violet said. "I'm learning to dodge Chloe's matchmaking attempts."

"Don't be so quick to ignore her, though." Darcy's eyes shone with love for her sister. "She did a good job in my case."

Chloe gasped. "Violet, I just had the perfect idea. Use the weekend trip you won at the auction as his gift. Take Jake up to our lake house this coming Saturday. Spend the day on the boat. Cook out."

"I can vouch for how romantic that is," Darcy said. "This weekend is yours if you want it."

Did she dare? Asking him to come spend the day with her would be agreeing to date him.

The sisters stared at her, waiting, looking hopeful.

"You can do this," Chloe whispered.

It was the push she needed. "Okay. I'll ask him. And if he won't go, then I'll have a weekend away by myself."

Chloe squealed her delight as Darcy hugged Violet. But their excitement didn't touch the anxiety tangling Violet's insides.

"Tell Jake we'll be available to babysit," Darcy said. "Our birthday gift to him."

"I can't thank you both enough."

But now, the problem would be finding the nerve to invite Jake. And if they stood any chance of having the type of relationship he was hinting at, she would have to share her complete past. Could she dare open up to him at the lake house on Saturday?

A knock sounded at Jake's back door. Probably Violet. She'd texted to say she planned to drop by on her way home from work.

Possibly to accept his invitation to go out?

He set down a freshly prepared bottle and, carrying Abby, quickly strode across the kitchen. He spotted Violet through the door and opened it with a smile.

She stood on his doorstep wearing navy slacks and a silky white blouse, her eyes shining with excitement. "Hi." She pushed her dark hair behind her ear as she glanced at Abby.

He was beginning to think her tucking the hair was a nervous habit because the wispy ends never stayed put.

With a pretty pink-cheeked blush, she leaned over and kissed Abby's head. "How'd our sweet girl do with the sitter today?"

Our sweet girl. Her words soothed his heart like the stroke of a soft-bristled paintbrush. Maybe everything he'd longed for wasn't out of reach after all. "Went great. Come on in."

She glanced at the kitchen table, where he'd set a bag of Chinese takeout.

"I don't want to keep you from your dinner. I just came by to accept your invitation for Friday. And to ask if you'd let me take you to the

O'Malleys' lake house for your birthday on Saturday. Darcy and Chloe volunteered to babysit." Her voice sounded breathy, as if she were nervous. But her warm hazel eyes still twinkled, radiating happiness.

She'd been thoughtful enough to remember his birthday and to make the arrangements. "I gladly accept. Tell Chloe and Darcy I'll be in touch."

"Fantastic." A small, pleased smile lifted the corners of her mouth.

He took her hand and tugged her toward him. "I ordered enough food for you. So no excuses."

With a laugh, she allowed him to pull her inside. "I am starving and was dreading making a frozen pizza."

"Then stay and eat with me. Would you mind feeding Abby while I set the table and get drinks?"

"I'd love to feed her."

He placed the baby in Violet's arms, and being so close made him want to feel her soft lips again.

Unable to resist, he lifted her chin and briefly, gently kissed her. Yes, her lips were just as warm and sweet as he remembered.

She sighed. "I've been thinking about that all day."

"Me, too." He winked at her, then went to retrieve the freshly made bottle.

While Violet fed Abby, the baby held onto her finger and looked into her eyes. The sight was so lovely, so precious, it made him ache. He wanted this, all of this—Violet and Abby and him together. A family.

Jake dragged himself from the daydream and grabbed plates, then poured iced tea.

When Abby finished, Violet put her in the bouncy seat. He sat adjacent to her at the small table for four and pulled the food containers out of the bag. "Mongolian beef or cashew chicken?"

"Both."

He laughed as he filled her plate and then his. "Chopsticks?"

"Of course."

"More power to you." With a grin, he handed them over. "Let's say a blessing."

She held out her hand, and he grasped it in his. Hers was delicate, warm, soft. Such gentle, capable hands, trained to tend to children. Hands that now brought a sense of peace to him.

He thanked God for the food and then added his gratitude for Violet and the way she had blessed Abby, the community...and him.

"Amen," he said.

"Amen," she whispered. When she looked up, she had tears in her eyes. "Thank you. I'm grateful, too. For you and for this town and how it's becoming a home for me." She looked down and brushed a finger over Abby's cheek. "And for this precious girl."

"I made an appointment with the lawyer for tomorrow afternoon."

Slowly, she drew in a deep breath and then, just as slowly, she let it out. "I'm glad. You've contacted Remy, given her multiple chances to come back. But I think Abby's permanence is important, and it's time to move toward that."

"So can I assume you won't be contacting Child Protective Services?"

She shook her head. "No. I feel sure your lawyer will handle everything properly. And I know Abby is in good hands."

"Before we know it, I'll—" Overwhelmed, he had to clear his constricted throat. "I'll be a dad."

Warmth shone in her eyes. Warmth and affection. "Yeah. And a good one, too. I'm so proud of how you've jumped in, learning to care for Abby."

Could that be love he saw in her eyes?

Abby kicked her feet, rattling the toys attached to the bouncy seat, startling them.

Violet laughed, and Jake couldn't resist leaning over and kissing her. "I love this. Being with my two favorite gals."

A soft knock sounded at the kitchen door, then it opened partway.

"Hello?" A head poked inside.

Jake's heart hit his knees. *No.*

Remy gave a weak smile and then her gaze darted straight to Abby. "Can I come in?"

As Jake leaped to his feet, scraping his chair legs across the floor, his chest squeezed so he could barely breathe. "Uh, yeah."

His cousin stepped inside and shut the door. She wore light blue scrubs and had a name badge hanging around her neck. This time, her hair looked clean and well-groomed and her eyes were bright and clear. "I'm sorry I didn't call first. I wasn't sure…" With a shrug, she let out a sigh. "I thought I knew what was best for Abigail, but now I think I made a mistake." She stared at her daughter with longing so intense it hurt him to look at Remy.

Jake wanted to grab Abby and take off, to just forget Remy had shown up.

At some point, Violet had taken Abby out of her seat and now stood by the table. She clutched the baby tightly to her chest.

Remy's gaze moved from Abby and landed on Violet. "You must be the pediatrician Jake mentioned. And also the woman who came with Jake looking for me at Dotty's Dippity-Do?"

She nodded, alarm in her eyes. "I'm Violet Crenshaw."

Jake couldn't believe Remy had shown up. Though he'd given Remy this last opportunity to claim Abby, he'd assumed she was still selfish and rebellious and wouldn't show. He wanted to rail against her return. Seeing the pain on Violet's face multiplied his own.

He stepped to Violet's side and put his arm around her waist, the two of them united as a team. Yet Remy hadn't mentioned taking Abby. Maybe he stood a chance. "You sound as if you're not sure what you want to do. I can tell you I'm *positive* what I want. I want to adopt Abby."

"Ever since you sent those photos of Abigail, I've doubted my decision. I started meeting with a counselor and got help from Florence Phillips from the shelter where I used to stay. I went to a weeklong parenting class in the evenings."

Why had he tried to entice Remy to come back? Why on earth hadn't he just gone straight to the lawyer as soon as he realized he loved Abby and was capable of caring for her?

"We've been happy," Jake said. "Abby is loved…no, adored, and is doing well. I… We… will take good care of your child."

A flash of the old Remy sparked in her eyes. "That's just it, Jake. She's *my* child. And I want her back."

Terror shot through him, making his stomach clench. How could he ever be assured Remy was off drugs? That she wouldn't get overwhelmed and take off again—leaving Abby in someone else's care?

He gripped Violet tighter, hoping she'd speak up, with personal as well as professional advice. But she remained rooted in place, holding Abby to her chest, patting the baby's back as if to comfort Abby as well as maybe herself.

Jake needed to get control of the situation. Needed to try to sound kind and understanding when every cell in him wanted to shout for Remy to get out. "Come sit down, and we can talk."

"I'm sorry, Jake. I know you've grown attached to Abigail…Abby. But you gave me a deadline, and I arrived before that deadline. I'm in a much better place now and want my baby back."

"You signed a paper."

"But nothing official."

"You deserted your daughter."

"I appreciate all you've done to help me. But now I'm back." She reached in a bag. "I totally understand your concerns. That's why I've brought copies of random drug tests I've had at my job and while I stayed at the shelter, proving I've been clean for over a year. Here's the rental agreement for the transitional housing I live in, showing I've been paying my rent. I also have a certificate for the parenting class I completed. Have pay stubs to show you I've been working full-time. And I have copies of my transcript so you can see I'm studying to become a certified nursing assistant."

As she set a thick file folder on the table, her gaze bore into his, determined. "There's also a list of phone numbers of everyone I associate with—counselor, teachers, boss, shelter director, pastor. I gave permission to tell you anything about me. Call them. Check on me." She drew in a deep breath, her nostrils flaring.

"Remy, come on," he said.

"I'm not confused anymore. I love my daughter and want her back." Remy walked over to Abby and rubbed her back. A strangled sob nearly choked her when she touched her child.

Desperate, Jake turned to the woman he loved who held the child he loved. "Violet?" His voice broke. He cleared his throat. "Can you please tell her I've been taking good care of Abby?"

"He has, Remy. Your daughter has been in good hands." Violet slipped out of his grasp. She turned to face him, looking into his eyes. Her bleak expression nearly brought him to his knees.

"I'm sorry, Jake. But I think Remy has shown she's changed and needs the opportunity to raise her daughter if she wants to."

Surely she hadn't just said those words. Surely he'd heard her wrong.

The tortured look in her eyes said otherwise.

She really did think he was wrong, and that Abby belonged with her mother.

He sucked in a breath, and shards of ice hacked at his nerve endings. "This is a family matter that's not any of your business. I think you should leave."

When Violet flinched, cold steel locked around his heart, walling off the hurt. He had to focus. Abby had to come first. He'd face Violet's betrayal later.

Violet gently placed the baby in Jake's arms. As she withdrew, her hand dragged along Abby's tummy, then legs, then off the tips of her toes, holding contact as long as possible.

Battling a sob, Jake realized his words had hurt Violet. But he didn't care. She'd turned on him when he needed her most.

"Remy, take good care of this precious girl," Violet said. Without another glance in Jake's direction, she slipped out the door, taking his heart with her.

"Jake?"

Think of Abby.

Remy blinked away tears, then held out her arms. "Please?"

When he hesitated, she reached in and gently took the baby. With tears running down her cheeks, she kissed Abby. Then she drew in a deep breath, as if trying to absorb the child's scent.

"You've ignored my emails," he said to his

cousin, trying to fight any sympathy he felt for her. "And from what we've gathered, you've been in an abusive situation. I won't let Abby live like that."

"Jake, I'm exhausted. Could I please stay here tonight? I'd like to spend some time getting reacquainted with Abigail. We can talk more in the morning."

What if Remy ran off during the night? But what other choice did he have? If he turned Remy away, she'd take Abby with her. "Yeah. But promise me you won't leave before we talk."

"I wouldn't do that to you."

"Promise me."

"I promise."

The problem was, he hadn't been able to trust Remy for years.

Now, he couldn't trust Violet, either.

Numb, Violet drove on autopilot, heading nowhere in particular. She just knew she couldn't sit in her house with Jake, Remy and Abby so close by.

An hour later, when she hit I-85, she steered her car onto the highway and headed north. She tried to concentrate on the latest article she'd read about antibiotic resistance. On the revised immunization schedule the CDC had put out in January. On the leaky faucet in the office bathroom.

Anything but Jake's hurtful words or the thought of Abby being taken from him.

She hated that she'd hurt him, but she'd had to do what she thought was right. Of course, she'd gotten entirely too close to the situation to start with. Had started to think of Abby as her child and Jake as…well, she might as well be honest with herself, as her husband. But he wasn't. And he'd made it clear she had no right to think that way.

She should have listened to her gut, should have avoided falling for him and Abby. How had she been so stupid, gotten so off track from focusing on her career goals? Was it because she missed home and having a family?

She kept driving north for more than an hour, heading out of Georgia into South Carolina. Ironically, toward…home.

When she reached the Greer exit, she took the ramp, crossed back over the highway, then drove five minutes to her parents' house. She had no clue what she would say to them. But even as dysfunctional as their relationship had been, she knew she needed to see them, to see her family.

She pulled up to the gated entrance and punched in the security code. After speaking to each other at her grandfather's funeral, her dad had started texting the code to her each time it changed, as if hoping Violet might one day return home. How many of those texts had she deleted, irritated at her father yet trying to ignore the pull they had on her?

But she had remembered each code until he'd send the next one.

The arm of the gate rose, allowing her to pass.

Massive homes lined curvy, landscaped streets. Old hardwoods and pines shaded the yards during the day. Now, after 9:00 p.m., outdoor lights discreetly lit driveways and perfectly manicured sidewalks. Violet drove to the back of the neighborhood, the older section where the homes sat on larger lots. Easing toward the front of her parents' traditional columned brick home, she sucked in a slow, deep breath, her heart pounding.

Not much had changed, except the trees had grown. The shrubs had filled in. She could remember climbing what used to be a small dogwood tree and having her mother come flying out the door to tell her to quit acting like a hooligan and get down, and her dad over in the driveway looking at her with a grin of approval.

Tears stung her eyes.

She eased to the curb in front of her neighbor's house, put the car in Park and turned the key. When she rolled down the windows, hot humid air rushed inside along with the sound of crickets and tree frogs. Memories assaulted her...

Being freshly bathed, wearing cool, cotton

pajamas, waiting up for her parents to arrive home so she could tell them about her boo-boo. And them making a fuss over it as they bandaged her knee and let her have ice cream after her bedtime… Having dinner at the "grown up table" in the formal dining room on Sunday afternoons after church, making her feel special… An impromptu picnic in the backyard, where her mom actually allowed them to eat only doughnuts and chocolate bars at Violet's request…

And then the fighting when she started dating Hank. Their shock and disappointment when she told them she was pregnant. Their manipulating to try to do damage control.

So many years had passed since then. More than a decade. Her son would be a teenager. And she'd missed it all, didn't know him at all.

She didn't even know her mom and dad anymore.

And they didn't know her.

She could simply get out of the car. Go ring the doorbell. Tell them she'd discovered that she needed family after all. She could explain to them how they'd hurt her when they made her give up her baby, but that she'd begun to learn God could turn things to good, that she'd like to try to let the past go and move on. But what she most wanted to tell them was that a certain man and precious baby had shown her what family could be like.

Unable to hold it at bay any longer, the pain of losing Jake and Abby rolled over her. As she leaned forward and sobbed, tears flowed down her cheeks onto the steering wheel.

Lord, why? Why allow me to fall in love with Jake and Abby only to rip them away from me?

Could she have done anything differently? Should she have supported Jake? Maybe, without her past, she would have taken his side. Maybe she'd let her past weigh too heavily on her decision to back Remy.

No, she truly believed that Remy had gotten her act together and deserved a chance at being a mother. If Violet had it to do over, she would say the same thing she'd said earlier to Jake.

Had Violet's parents agonized like this? Camilla had told Jake they wanted to apologize, they regretted their decision. Would they make the same decision again if faced with a pregnant teen daughter?

A rumbling sound started in the back of the house and grew louder. Her dad appeared, wheeling the trash bin to the end of the driveway. Violet sucked in her breath and held it, fearing he might spot her before she was prepared to go in.

"Buford, are you still out there?" her mother called from the side porch door.

Hearing her voice…Violet pressed a hand to her lips, holding in a sudden sob.

"Yes," her dad answered. "Setting out the garbage can."

He'd probably also spent time puttering in the garden by moonlight.

"Your answering service is on the phone."

"Be right there." Shaking his head, he hurried back up the driveway to the house, where he would check in with the hospital and probably rush off to perform surgery, like a million nights before.

Violet's heart ached. Her head ached. And now her stomach churned.

She couldn't go in there and see them right now. Not in the shape she was in tonight.

What she needed right now wouldn't be found in the Crenshaw home. She needed time to heal, time to regain her strength before contacting her parents.

Why had she let herself think for a minute that Jake and Abby could fill the massive void in her life? Now she only had one option.

Forget Jake.

Forget the way his beard had tickled her lips the first time they'd kissed, the way his deep blue eyes sparkled when he laughed, the way his hands looked so big and strong yet at the same time gentle as he held Abby.

Violet sniffed and wiped her eyes. She'd been a fool. Everything had blown up in her face, as she'd feared. It was time to go back into self-protect mode. She needed to pour herself into her work. To grow her practice. Make a name for herself in Appleton. Help children who needed her—not a baby who'd settle in her arms as if Violet were her mother, not a baby who'd steal her heart.

She started the car and pulled away from the curb without looking back.

Total focus on her career would fill this gaping emptiness.

It had to.

Chapter Eleven

Jake woke with a start at 5:00 a.m. An odd sound had roused him. Had it been through the baby monitor?

Remy.

He bolted from bed, throwing on clothes as he rushed across the hallway, his heart thudding in his chest.

In Abby's room, Remy sat on the bed holding the baby, feeding her a bottle.

Jake threw one hand against the door frame to steady himself while mashing the other hand against his raging heartbeat. "I can't believe I didn't hear you in the kitchen making the bottle."

"You're probably exhausted from working and watching Abigail."

"We've been calling her Abby for a while now." His tone sounded combative, but maybe it should. He felt as if he were going to battle for Abby's welfare.

"I like it. It fits."

He wanted to tell her the nickname wasn't her choice any longer since she'd abandoned her daughter. But he needed to calm down. He had to talk Remy into letting him adopt Abby.

The baby slurped down the last of the formula. Remy lifted her to her shoulder and burped her.

"Look, Remy. We need to talk."

Guilt flashed in her eyes. "Actually, I need to get back for work. Could you please help me gather Abigail—Abby's—things?"

Hands fisted at his sides, he sucked in a shaky breath. "You said we could talk."

"I know. I'm sorry. But I realized I shouldn't rush back. I need time to get Abby settled at the day-care center before my shift." Her eyes saddened. "If I delay, it'll just make it tougher for you."

"Then you know how attached I've gotten to her. I love her, Remy. You can't just take off with her like this."

"Jake, I appreciate all you've done for her... and for me." Her eyes hardened, like the stubborn, rebellious Remy of the past. "But Abby is my child, and I'm ready to be her mother."

"How can you suddenly be ready to be a mother? Just a couple of weeks ago, you looked strung out and dumped her on me without so much as a phone number. You have no right to—"

"I was not strung out. I was worn-out, frazzled

and feeling like the worst mother ever because she wouldn't stop crying. But now I'm more prepared for motherhood. My postpartum depression is gone." She stood and placed Abby in her car seat, carefully buckling her in.

"What about the drugs? What about the abusive boyfriend, who I assume is Abby's father?"

Remy grabbed piles of Abby's clothes and stuffed them in a piece of luggage that she must've brought with her. "I showed you the drug tests. I'm really and truly clean. And I was telling the truth when I told you Abby's father died."

"Then why were you at a shelter?"

"Because he never did get off drugs and I needed to get away from him. He died of an overdose before she was born. That's when I moved out of the shelter into my apartment."

"So you're still living in transitional housing? Is it safe?"

"Yes. It's about thirty minutes north of Atlanta, so I'm closer to you." She snatched up her purse, pulled out a piece of paper and held it out to him. "I wrote down all my contact information for you this time. You're welcome to come visit us anytime."

"What about all her things?" Helplessly, he pointed to the travel bed and bouncy seat.

"I'll take that bouncer and new car seat, but

for now, let's leave the bed and changing table here for when we visit you, okay?"

No, it wasn't okay. But short of calling the police, there was no way he could stop Remy because he'd never filed for legal custody, had never taken the letter she wrote to a lawyer to find out if it was legally binding.

And it probably wasn't. Not now that she wanted Abby back.

If only Violet was here, maybe she could calmly talk some sense into Remy. But no, Violet would probably be helping usher Remy and Abby out the door.

He raked a hand through his hair. He needed to think straight. If he couldn't stop Remy, what did Abby need? "What about her formula?"

"I already packed it, along with her bottles and diapers. Thank you for buying her everything I forgot to pack when I brought her here. I'll pay you back."

"I don't want your money," he snapped. "I want you to do what's best for Abby."

Her face softened. She reached out and touched his arm. "Don't you see, Jakey? That's what I'm trying to do. As soon as I decided I wanted to raise Abby, I started trying to be more like you, the guy I've always looked up to, the dependable one."

Jakey. She hadn't called him that since they were kids.

She lifted the baby carrier in one hand, then reached for the suitcase with the other.

With his chest squeezing so tightly he couldn't take a deep breath, he stepped in, lifted the bag and followed her out into the dewy, dark morning to her beat-up sedan. "I need to get you the car seat base."

Once he installed it in the center of the backseat, Remy clicked the carrier into place. "You want to tell her bye?"

"You need to keep her on that new lactose-free formula, otherwise her stomach hurts."

"I will."

"And the yellow pacifier is her favorite."

With a pained expression, Remy nodded. "Anything else I should know?"

"If she cries at night, try swaddling her. If she cries while you're holding her, then she does better if you hold her so she can see your face."

Tears pooled in her eyes. "I'll remember all that. Thank you. I'll take good care of her."

"Promise me that if you decide you can't handle it, you'll come to me. Okay?"

"Okay."

"Promise me."

"I promise."

He squeezed in the backseat beside Abby, who was lit only by the moon and the dim car light. He rubbed his thumb over her soft cheek. "I'll see you later, sweet girl."

Abby stared at him, bright-eyed and happy.

He kissed her forehead, taking time to breathe in her powdery fragrance. "I love you." His throat convulsed, so he yanked himself out of the car and stormed inside before he made a fool of himself.

Other than his parents, Jake had never told another living soul he loved them. Now he loved Abby, and she'd been torn away from him.

He needed Violet, the other person he'd loved, the only one who had the power to comfort him now. But after the way she'd turned on him, he'd never be able to trust her again.

Two days. Two long, *miserable* days. Two days without seeing or hearing from Jake.

Violet had thought he would cool down and call by now. But he'd been silent…and absent.

Remy's car had left sometime Tuesday between 1:00 a.m. when Violet returned from her parents' house and 6:00 a.m. when she went out for her run. So Violet had to assume she'd left with the baby.

Her heart contracted, a pain so intense she clutched her arms in front of her and laid her head on her desk.

Poor Jake. He must be devastated.

He apparently hadn't come around to believing Remy needed a chance to raise Abby, so he most likely wasn't going to forgive Violet. He must feel she betrayed him.

She missed him. Missed his smile, his laugh, his loyalty.

But he'd told her to butt out of family matters. She needed to remember that part, as well. Needed to forget and move on.

Somehow.

Work. Burying herself in work. And in prayer. It was the only way she'd been able to get by for the past two days.

"Hey."

Violet jerked upward, her face burning at being caught with tears on her cheeks. Chloe stood at the office door.

"I'm sorry to interrupt. Your receptionist let me come on back."

Violet motioned her inside. "You caught me… resting."

Sitting in the chair facing the desk, Chloe leaned across, placing a hand on Violet's arm. "I heard Remy came for Abby."

"How'd you hear?"

"I ran into Jake. He's pretty torn up."

Violet drew in a shuddering breath, blinking away a fresh wave of tears. Abby was definitely gone. Would Violet see her again? "I don't know how he's going to recover from this."

Chloe winced. "You really think Remy's turned her life around?"

"I do. She brought evidence that she has."

Chloe reached for Violet's hand and squeezed. "I know you're hurting about Abby. But why are you avoiding Jake?"

"What did he tell you?"

"Just that the two of you had a difference of opinion, and he hadn't seen you in a couple of days."

With a sigh, Violet leaned back in her chair. "Yeah, a difference of opinion, all right."

"Over…?"

"Besides the fact we don't agree on Remy's right to raise her child? Well, for starters, he told me to butt out of a family matter."

Chloe frowned. "Well, I'm sure he was upset, acting out of fear of losing Abby."

Violet's stomach fluttered. That's what she had told herself a dozen times. "Maybe. But I'd let down my guard for the first time in my adult life. I thought we had feelings for each other. Then as soon as things got tough, he pushed me away, shut me out."

"Because you thought Remy should raise her daughter?"

"Yeah. When Jake refused to give Abby to Remy and mentioned adopting her, I stood up for Remy."

Chloe's nose scrunched. "Ouch. The man probably felt you'd stabbed him in the back. Was probably acting in self-defense."

Violet pressed her hands to her hot cheeks. "Even though it's not what I want, it's what I thought was right."

"Right for who?"

Violet's shoulders dropped. "For Remy. And given the fact she wants her daughter and is in a good place now, then for Abby, as well."

Eyes wide with surprise, Chloe shook her head. "Well, I think you need to talk to him. Explain your feelings—which, frankly, puzzle me. After working with Jake so closely, and knowing Remy's history, how could you have sided with Remy? Jake was the good guy here."

"It's complicated and…private."

When Violet didn't offer more, Chloe stood, her blue eyes stricken. "Oh, okay. Well, maybe you'll feel comfortable talking about it someday."

"Thanks for understanding. And for coming to check on me." The hurt on Chloe's face made Violet's throat ache. But she felt she couldn't tell anyone else about her past if she hadn't first told Jake. "I'm sorry I can't tell you more right now."

Chloe came around the desk and hugged Violet. "I want you to go ahead and use the lake house this weekend. Get away for a while to heal. Then later this summer, you can use it again when you're feeling more like having fun."

"Thanks, Chloe. You're a good friend."

Yes, getting away would be good. She'd have

her calls forwarded. Would go to the lake house on Friday evening and spend two glorious days on the water, deciding what to do about Jake. And whether to tell him about her son.

If she told him, would he then understand why she took Remy's side?

Jake wiped sweat off his brow with his sleeve. With the Emerson house having fixtures installed, he'd poured himself into the Bonner project all week. They'd just finished the rough framing, and he'd enjoyed pounding some nails, straining his muscles, trying to hold at bay the ache and sadness.

With a sigh, he loaded the last of the tools in the back of his truck. The framers had left the work site, and it was nearly dark. Time to quit delaying and head home.

Home to quiet. A quiet that held no peace anymore. Without Abby and Violet, the house just seemed empty and lonely.

He'd called Remy every day to check on Abby. She said they were doing fine. But he had no idea how Violet was doing.

He and Violet were supposed to be out on their first date right now to celebrate his moving to adopt Abby. Shutting his eyes, he battled the pain that had been lashing at him since Monday night.

A red truck pulled up behind Jake's, and Zeb climbed out.

Oh, man. Anytime anyone acted sympathetic, he could hardly hold it together.

Jake held out his hand to shake. "Hey. What are you doing here?"

"Stopped by to check on you."

"Check on me?" Clenching his teeth together, he prepared.

Zeb squinted his eyes, giving Jake a look of pity. "Heard about Remy taking the baby. I'm sorry, man."

Jake couldn't look at his friend. He stared at gravel they'd put down in the driveway area, scraping at it with the toe of his boot. "Yeah, well…thanks."

Zeb rested an arm along the edge of the truck bed. "So whadya doing to help your doctor girl-friend through this?"

Jake's gaze flew to Zeb's. "We're not together."

"The doc seemed attached to the little gal. Figured she must be hurtin' as bad as you."

Jake steeled himself against the pain he'd tried to push away all week. "Violet sided with Remy over raising Abby."

"Well, a woman is entitled to her opinion. Could be you're being hardheaded, you know."

For the first time in days, one corner of Jake's mouth tilted up in a partial smile. He lifted a brow. "Me? Hardheaded?"

"What makes a man a good contractor can get him in trouble with the ladies."

"Speaking from experience?"

"Could be." Zeb squinted up at the full moon, a hint of a smile tugging at his lips. "Sure would be a shame to mess up with the doc over something that's hurt both of you."

The man made a good point. "What makes you such an expert?"

"Forty years of marriage and several nights in the doghouse." With a wave, Zeb climbed in his truck, shut the door and stuck his head out the open window. "See you back here when you're ready for my crew."

Jake shook his hand. "Thanks for stopping by."

"Don't make it a wasted trip."

With a shake of his head and a smile, Jake strode to his truck and climbed in. Time was 9:00 p.m. He and Violet would have been out celebrating right now. And tomorrow, heading to the lake for his birthday.

Would she still go?

Lord, I need Your help here. Please ease the hurt and help me do what's right.

Please watch over Abby.

And over Violet. I haven't prayed for her through all this, and Zeb's right. She must be hurting, too.

The phone vibrated in his hand. It showed

Remy's name on the screen. His heart raced as he quickly swiped his finger to answer.

"Hey. Is Abby okay?"

The baby cried in the background. "Yeah. She's fine. No fever or anything. She's just fussy."

Hearing her cries sucked the oxygen out of him. "Do you need me to come?"

"No. I just can't remember what you told me she likes when she's fussy. I tried putting her in the baby carrier against my chest to snuggle her. Then tried holding her so she could see my face."

"She likes to be swaddled in the striped hospital blanket. It's the only one that seems to hold her tight enough. Did you take it with you?"

"Hang on, let me check."

Jake waited what seemed like an eternity with Abby's cries moving away from the phone, then coming back in close range. It was all he could do not to head the truck toward Atlanta to Remy's apartment.

"It's here," she said. "Thanks, I'll give that a try."

"Call me back if she won't calm down. She may be sick."

"Okay."

"I'm serious. I can drive down there in a flash."

Remy sighed, Abby's colicky crying nearly

drowning it out. "I promise you I want a happy, healthy baby, Jake. So please don't worry."

They said their goodbyes and hung up. But he couldn't get Abby's cries out of his head.

Should he file to try to take custody? Would he have any grounds to stand on? Maybe he should call an attorney in the morning.

By the time he'd arrived at his house, he'd decided to make that call. He walked inside and turned on the family room light.

His cell phone buzzed. Remy again. "Everything okay?"

"Listen," Remy said. "Blessed quiet."

She was right. The only thing he could hear was the sound of the blood whooshing in his ears from the fright of seeing her name on his screen again. As his heart rate returned to normal, he let out a long, silent breath. "I'm glad the blanket worked," he said.

"Thanks for suggesting it. I knew you'd worry if I didn't call back."

"I appreciate that. It's tough not being in control."

"Believe me, I know. And I'll try to make the transition as easy on you as possible."

Standing just outside the dark kitchen, he rested his head against the cool wood of the built-in cabinet. "Thanks."

"I'm going to do this, you know. I'm going to make you believe in me."

Tears stung his eyes. "I believed in you all along, Rem. As long as you were clean, I knew you'd come back. I just lost track of that when I fell in love with Abby, with this idea of the perfect family."

"You wanted that ideal family we never had because I messed it up."

Sure, he'd blamed her when he was a teen. But she hadn't had an easy road. "I guess we all got dealt some blows and did the best we could."

"I love you, Jakey. Thanks for always looking out for me."

His throat clenched tight and wouldn't let go. He swallowed. "I love you, too. Kiss Abby for me."

"I will. 'Night."

Jake slipped outside and went to sit on the old swing, where he'd spent time with Abby, trying to soothe her. Looking over at Violet's dark house, he wondered why she had jeopardized their relationship by pulling away from him and supporting Remy.

Because honestly, now that he thought back to that evening, if Violet had said nothing, the outcome would have been the same.

Why had she risked their love like that, knowing how much her betrayal would hurt him?

He should ask her. Because he needed to know, if nothing else, to have closure.

Taking a deep breath, he pushed up out of the swing and went back inside.

He wouldn't contact her yet. He'd pray about it tonight and make a decision in the morning.

Chapter Twelve

Violet's hand hovered over her cell phone, her fingers trembling with indecision.

She sat on the big front porch at the O'Malleys' lake house, surrounded by woods and glistening lake water, with her phone resting on the wide wooden arm of a rocking chair. She'd been rocking and thinking since she'd finished her morning coffee. For the past hour, as the sun had risen over the lake, she'd gone back and forth on whether to call Jake.

Yes, I'll do it. For about the fourteenth time, she started to hit the call button. Yet something made her hesitate. Again.

Anger and hurt and longing all jumbled into a mess inside her, making her feel more alone than ever.

She had no one. No one who knew her inside and out.

Actually…she did.

God, it's me again. I don't know what to do.

A tired sigh slipped out. *I can't do this anymore. I can't do this all by myself. I've made a mess of every relationship in my life. I need You to take over.*

She leaned her head against the chair cushion, closed her eyes and rocked, back and forth, back and forth. As the chair runners made a steady creaking sound on the wooden porch, a sense of peace washed over her. No more pretense of being in control. No trying to bend her life to fit her own will.

She needed to trust God to lead her.

The sound of tires on gravel jerked her eyes open. Who was coming down the private dirt road at this hour?

The sight of Jake's truck sent her heart into a gallop as she hopped up from the chair. She sucked in a breath and held it as he parked and got out.

He looked haggard, as if he hadn't slept since she'd last seen him. But his broad shoulders, rugged beard and piercing blue eyes still made her knees weak.

When he reached the bottom of the steps, he stopped and looked up to the porch. "Violet."

She couldn't read anything from his guarded expression.

"Hi, Jake."

"Can I join you?"

His soft request, the hesitancy of his words, closed her throat. She gestured to the chair beside her.

He climbed the steps and moved past her, filling the space around her with his wide shoulders and his clean, woodsy scent. Simply having him there made her feel...right, less alone.

She could barely look at him for fear she'd burst into tears. Was this an answer to her prayer? Was there still a chance for them?

He turned the other rocking chair so it faced hers. He sat and leaned his elbows on his knees, hands clasped. "I figured we should talk about what happened."

"Okay."

"I have questions. I need to figure out where you were coming from."

That sounded encouraging, as if maybe he was willing to listen and consider her side.

But could she trust him with all of her past? "You told me to stay out of your family business. Have you changed your mind?"

His deep blue eyes softened with regret. "I'm sorry. I was distraught over having Abby taken from me. And when you didn't jump in to back me up...well, I lashed out."

"I understood that, but it still hurt. More than anything, I—" Tears threatened, and she blinked them away. "I wanted to feel like part of a close family. You and Abby gave me that."

Reaching out, he brushed his work-roughened hand over hers, soothing her.

Her heart twisted. No matter what she told herself, no amount of work could make her forget Jake. Nothing could.

"I felt the same thing," he said. "Then Remy showed up and blew our bubble of happiness to smithereens."

"Jake—"

"No, let me finish. I don't want to cut you out of my life. But I need to know why you sided with Remy. Because if you cared for me like I thought you did, you wouldn't have hurt me that way."

"Jake…"

He held up a hand. "I think there's more going on, and it's time you trust me enough to tell me."

If she had any hope of a relationship with Jake, she had to tell him, tell him everything. So he'd understand.

Jake studied Violet's beautiful, troubled eyes.

He took her hand in his and sat knee to knee, encouraging her. "Tell me. From the beginning."

She intertwined her fingers with his, gripping his hand firmly. "All my life, I'd planned to be a doctor. From the time I got my first toy medical kit, I wanted to be a surgeon like my dad, to make him proud."

"I didn't realize he's a doctor, too."

She nodded. "He and mom were prominent in the community. Had high expectations for their only child. And I wanted to be that girl—that perfect girl, with perfect grades, making a name for herself, saving the world."

"Looks like you did that." As soon as the words left his mouth, pain flashed in her eyes.

Then he knew her life hadn't gone as her parents had planned.

"When I was a senior in high school, I...I got pregnant."

He sucked in a breath. "Oh, man."

An ironic laugh puffed out of her. "I'd been such a good girl. But the older I got, the more pressured I felt to live up to my parents' expectations. I decided I wanted to have some fun."

"Let me guess. You went for the bad boy."

"Not so much that. He was just...intense. Gave one hundred and ten percent in everything he did—including relationships. He was fun and attentive, was wildly popular, made me feel beautiful and desirable. We were this perfect couple, and I thrived on that new, exciting reputation.

"As we applied to colleges and talked of the future, he told me he needed to know I was committed to him. And needed to know I really loved him. Despite my upbringing and beliefs, I fell for that line. I thought, finally, I had control over some part of my life my parents couldn't touch, and I made a stupid choice."

She sighed and tried to let go of his hand, but he held on.

"It was so clichéd," she said. "We were together one time, and I became pregnant. He freaked and dumped me, claiming the child wasn't his. Which was such a joke. Not one person believed him."

"Violet, I'm so sorry."

"Apparently, he couldn't do one hundred and ten percent on fatherhood." She laughed, but it held no humor.

"So I had to tell my parents, who didn't react well. They then went into protect-the-family-name mode."

Jake pulled their clasped hands to his chest, offering support.

"They were horrified. Ashamed. Right after graduation, they whisked me off to my aunt and uncle's house in Alabama to try to cut down on gossip because by then I was showing. The next thing I knew, they had found this really nice, childless couple eager to adopt."

"So you decided to give up the baby?"

She gazed into his eyes, and the pain he saw there squeezed the air out of his lungs.

"I wanted to keep him. Once I could feel my baby moving, I imagined keeping him, my parents helping me raise him."

"Obviously, they didn't allow that."

"They told me I was being ridiculous, that I couldn't support a baby on my own. That I would never achieve my dream of being a surgeon. I begged them to help me. I told them I would go to college locally. Then we could figure out medical school later."

Tears pooled at the edges of her eyes, wetting her eyelashes, making them dark and spiky. He wanted to hug her, hold her, tell her he wished he could take the pain away. Yet he knew she needed to share it, so he would finally, truly know her.

He wiped a thumb under her eyes to brush away the tears. "Go on."

"They refused to help raise the baby or to even help financially. Said if I kept the child, they would cut me off. My aunt and uncle sided with my parents. My grandparents wanted to help but wouldn't go against my parents."

"So you were on your own."

"Yes. And I was afraid I couldn't do it."

"You were a kid yourself, Violet. It would have been nearly impossible to raise a child, attend college and medical school and support yourself financially."

"But I wish I had," she whispered.

The tears broke loose and poured down her cheeks, bringing him to his feet. He wrapped her into his arms and let her cry against his chest.

She poured out her hurt, wetting his shirt. When the crying stopped, she went inside for a tissue. He followed her and pulled her beside him on the couch.

She sniffed and dabbed at her eyes. "I'm sorry."

"Don't be."

"I usually keep a tighter rein on my emotions."

"I'm glad you told me." He scooted closer so he could touch her. Holding on to her hands, he gave her a gentle smile. "So the baby was a boy?"

"Yes. I never got to hold him. But I've always imagined cradling him in my arms, smelling his unique baby scent."

"And you ended up going into pediatrics."

"Yeah. Once I had the baby, I left Alabama and went straight to college. Cut off all communication with my parents. Refused to let them control another minute of my life."

"I'm sorry you experienced all that pain."

"I've never gotten over giving him up. Never gotten over the guilt of putting my selfish ambition before him. Never gotten over being so weak I let them make the decision."

"You were barely eighteen. I think they probably should have made the decision for you."

"Though I know in my head it was probably best for my son, I still wish I'd been brave enough to step out on my own to raise him. Like you jumped in to take care of Abby despite your inexperience. You did the honorable thing."

Jake threw his hand up in protest. "Whoa, don't say that. Violet, your act of giving up your son to a loving home was just as honorable. If raising a child had kept you from finishing medical school, you wouldn't be helping so many children today."

She rested her head against his shoulder. "Thank you for saying that. After watching you struggle caring for Abby, I can see how difficult it would have been. Just like it's been difficult for Remy."

"And that's why you sided with her."

Leaning back, she gave him a sad smile. "Yeah. She'd proven she was ready to care for Abby. I think she deserves at least a chance if she wants it." Her brow furrowed.

"What is it?"

"I actually think—"

He brushed a hair back from her face. "Go ahead. I want to know."

"Maybe my opinion is colored by my experience. But I think you should ask your cousin to move back to Appleton and offer to help with Abby while Remy finishes school and gets a job. She could use family nearby to support her."

The idea settled inside him like two perfectly dovetailed joints. "You're one smart woman, Violet Crenshaw."

A smile slowly bloomed on her face. "I try to be."

"You know, I think your parents loved you and did what they thought best at the time. Maybe it's time to respond to their calls. Time to rebuild that relationship, so you'll have more support."

Resignation—and possibly determination—sparked in her eyes. "You're pretty smart yourself, Jake West."

"So that's a yes?"

"That's a maybe...leaning toward a yes. I've had their phone number pulled up on my phone off and on all week. I just couldn't quite hit Call."

"I believe you can do it. And *need* to do it to fully heal."

She blinked at moisture in her eyes. "Maybe now that I've dumped it all on you, I can move forward and learn to forgive."

"I'm proud of you, proud of how you've overcome a painful past. And I understand why you spoke up for Remy." Jake was quickly falling for this brave, strong woman. A woman who was kind and fair and generous, even though she had been through so much.

He lifted her chin and looked into her eyes. "I've missed you like crazy."

"I've missed you, too."

He glanced at her rosy, full lips and slowly—

She gasped. "Wait." Hopping up, she hurried

outside. A moment later, the car door slammed. Then she reappeared inside.

Her face full of joy, she set a gift wrapped in bright blue-and-green-striped paper in his lap. "Happy birthday."

"A present for me?"

"Open it."

As he ran his finger carefully under the tape, trying not to tear the paper, she leaned toward him, eyes sparkling, hands clasped in front of her as if dying to help. Her childlike excitement was contagious.

He could imagine her at Christmas. "As a child, you ripped off the wrapping paper and tossed it aside, making quick work of all your presents, didn't you?"

"How'd you know?"

"Because it's about to kill you that I'm taking so long."

Her laugh was like music to his ears. "You know me too well. Now, can you, just this once, live dangerously and tear it right off?"

Yes, he finally knew her fully. And he liked everything about her.

With a quick yank, he tore off the paper. He drew in a breath. She'd given him a photo album filled with photos of Abby. Photos Violet had taken of him with Abby. Photos he'd taken of Violet with Abby. A photo Chloe had taken of the three of them at church.

He ran his fingers over a photo of Abby sleeping, sucking her thumb. "When did you put all this together?"

"Last Sunday night after I found out the date of your birthday."

"What if I hadn't shown up today?"

Large, sad eyes gazed into his. "I was going to keep it."

He placed the book on the coffee table. Then he ran his hands through her hair and cupped her cheeks. "Being with you has made this the best birthday ever."

When his lips touched hers, he once again savored the sense of belonging he'd longed for his whole life. He loved Violet and wanted a life with her.

But one fear nagged at the back of his mind, preventing him from saying the words. If Violet couldn't mend the relationship with her parents, would his love be enough? Would she ever heal enough to return his love?

Jake might only get one chance to do this right. So with Violet by his side, he drove toward Remy's apartment after church on Sunday, mentally preparing himself.

He wouldn't get angry if she said no. He'd simply persuade her that it was in her best interest.

"I'm going to stay calm and not lose patience."

Violet set her hand on his knee, a reassuring gesture. "Unless Remy's school credits don't transfer, or she can't find a job in Appleton, I don't think she'll refuse. She loves you and respects you."

He laughed. "How could you tell she feels that way from the brief meeting at my house?"

"I know the man you are. Honorable..." Her cheeks flushed pink, and she looked away. "Lovable."

"Thanks for coming with me today." He covered her hand with his.

"I wouldn't miss a chance to see Abby. Or to cheer you on."

Following his cell phone's directions, they ended on a dead-end street lined with duplexes that all looked alike. They pulled up to the curb in front of her tiny unit.

"Looks well maintained," Violet said.

"Not bad." Looked better than he expected, at least on the outside.

He went around to Violet's side and helped her out. They walked to the front door and knocked.

Remy opened the door. His gaze went straight to Abby, held snugly in her mother's arms. "She looks beautiful, perfect."

"Hi, Remy," Violet said.

"Can I hold her?" he asked.

Smiling, Remy handed her over. "She's missed you. Come on in."

The baby looked at his face, and he thought

she seemed happy to see him. With the precious bundle in the crook of his elbow, he beamed at Violet and Remy. "I've missed her. Thanks for letting us come by."

"Anytime. Y'all sit down."

"You have a nice apartment," Violet said.

Jake looked around as he took a seat on the couch. Sparse secondhand furniture. But clean and tidy. Lots of sunlight streaming in the front window as well as from a window in the small, adjoining kitchen.

Clean bottles lined the countertop, drying upside down on paper towels.

"Thanks, Violet. It's a project of Peace House, provided for former residents along with job training. I pay rent each month according to how much I make, and we can stay here for up to eighteen months."

"Sounds like a great program." His gaze met Violet's. *Lord, please let Remy agree to move home.*

"So how is everything going with Abby?" Violet asked.

"I'm exhausted, but she seems to be doing fine. She's eating better. Crying less as I'm learning to relax. And is bonding with the child-care workers."

Jake's heart felt bruised. He wanted Abby with him, at least some of the time. "Where are you working?"

Abby started to fuss, and Remy hopped up, grabbed a pacifier and popped it in her mouth.

"I'm still working full-time at a doctor's office, and going to school part-time. Like I said the other day, I'm studying to be a certified nursing assistant." Pride gleamed in her expression, and for the first time since she was about fifteen, he saw a glimpse of the Remy he remembered from their early childhood.

"I'm happy for you."

"Jake, I know you're still concerned about Abby because of the way I acted when I left her with you, but I'm not that woman anymore."

"It's okay," he said. "After fumbling my way through, believe me, I understand."

She swatted at tears. "Sorry. I've worked really hard to pull myself together. I'm determined to be a good mom, to do right by her."

"You should be proud," Violet said.

Jake knew the memories probably hurt Violet, but she was generous in her praise. And he admired her even more.

"I am proud of myself. But mostly, I'm grateful to both of you for watching out for my baby."

Jake leaned forward and took his cousin's hand. "Come home to Appleton, Remy. The local technical college has a CNA program, and there are job openings at the hospital. You can live with me until you're done with school and can afford to move out on your own. Either that or let me help you with your own place until you're able to do it alone."

Her gaze darted from him to Violet, uncertainty drawing her brows downward.

"You'll have a built-in pediatrician," Violet said with a reassuring smile. "And babysitters who are ready and willing and will love your girl as much as you do."

"Are y'all getting married or something?" Remy asked.

Jake's neck heated and was probably as red as Zeb's truck. He laughed, but it sounded more like a rusty gate creaking open. "Well, we haven't talked that far ahead. But we'll both be there to help you."

He couldn't bring himself to look at Violet. She was probably mortified, maybe even angry about his reaction.

"Remy, we promise not to interfere," Violet said, "or to try to take over Abby's care. Right, Jake?"

He glanced at Violet. She didn't seem disturbed by Remy's embarrassing question or his choked response. "That's right. We're offering assistance, not trying to step into your place."

"Why?" Remy asked.

"Because you deserve a chance," Violet said simply.

Jake's throat tightened as if caught in a monkey wrench. The woman he loved never had a chance with her own child, yet she'd been strong enough to stand up to him, causing herself pain, because she wanted to give Remy the opportunity Violet had never had.

"Thank you both for the offer." A smile quivered on Remy's lips. "I'll investigate the possibility of transferring my college credits. I'll seriously consider moving home."

Relief swamping him, Jake reached for Violet's hand.

Violet swiped tears from her eyes and then gave him a watery smile. A laugh burst out of her. "I may not be family, but I hope the next time someone asks whether we're getting married, you won't look like you've swallowed a two-by-four."

"Ooh, she nailed you, cuz," Remy said with a chuckle.

Tugging at Violet's hand, he scooted her closer and planted a big kiss on her lips. "Later...we need to talk."

Violet pulled her cell phone out of her pocket and held it up. "First, I need to make a phone call. You two have inspired me, and it's time to finally call my parents."

"Do you need me?"

"No, I'm good. You, Remy and Abby enjoy your visit."

As Violet slipped outside, Jake knew he'd found the woman he would spend his life with.

Maybe they'd even be blessed with children of their own.

"Why's Violet calling her parents?" Remy asked.

"They've been at odds since she was in high school."

Reaching for her cell phone, Remy took a deep breath. "Maybe it's time for me to do the same. I have a lot of apologizing to do."

"Paul has been looking for you. And Edith is dying to see Abby. They'll be relieved to hear from you, but be patient with them."

She stood. "Are you okay here with Abby while I go call?"

"Are you kidding? Take your time. And, hey, tell them I plan to bring Violet down there soon and that they're going to love her."

He couldn't imagine being any happier. Well, except for the possibility of having that talk with Violet later.

It was time to tell her he loved her, and he hoped she'd be able to return those feelings.

"Hi, Mom. It's me."

Violet couldn't sit still on the front porch, so she hopped up and took off down Remy's driveway.

Her mother gasped. "Violet? It's really you?"

Taking a right at the end of the driveway, she ambled down the sidewalk. "Yes. I've been thinking of you and Daddy. Wanted to see how you're doing."

"Why, we're fine, dear. It's so good to hear your voice. How are you?"

"I'm okay… Great, actually."

"I'm glad."

Tense silence reverberated in her ear. Why had she called?

"I'm so sorry, Violet," her mom whispered. "*We're* sorry. Sorry that we weren't there for you when you needed us."

A crushing ache squeezed her chest. Suddenly feeling weak-kneed, she headed toward a picnic table in a small park at the corner.

"I shouldn't have shut you out," Violet said. "I've realized lately that you probably only did what you thought best."

"Yes, we truly did love you and think it was best for you. We feared you couldn't manage since you'd never babysat or held down a full-time job. You were idealistic and had no idea what you'd be getting into. But, honey, we should have listened to what you wanted. Should have worried less about what other people thought."

"Is that why you've been trying to contact me?"

"Yes. To apologize. To try to make amends. Although we know it's too late to change the past, we'd like to heal from our losses. Honey, our lives have been empty without you."

Tears stung her eyes. "I've been helping my... uh, neighbor take care of his three-week-old niece lately, and I see how much work it is. I realized I would have had a tough time on my own."

"Well, we could have helped you raise our grandson. We let our own pride as well as our dreams of you becoming a surgeon, following in Dad's footsteps, get in the way. We've experienced regret over the years."

"I think my son's probably had a good life." She hated the uncertainty in her voice.

"I'm sure he has. He went to a wonderful family who'd tried for years to have a child and wanted him desperately. I promise you, we checked them out thoroughly."

Relief washed over her. Though she had assumed as much—because her parents were nothing if not thorough—she'd still had moments of doubt and fear.

A comfortable moment passed without either of them speaking. She enjoyed knowing her mother was on the other end of the line, such a normal thing that many people took for granted.

"Are y'all in good health? Still playing tennis each week?"

"Your dad had a little scare with his heart a

couple of years ago, but he's fine now. And yes, we still play tennis at the club. Although these days we're in a senior league."

Camilla's voice soothed Violet, reminding her of childhood. So much wasted time. If only she'd called sooner. So much pain because of her stubbornness. "I'm sorry I shut y'all out. I've been pigheaded."

Her mother laughed, but it was mixed with tears. Then she blew her nose. "Well, you do have your dad's genes."

"And yours." At the sound of her mother's chuckle, decade-old pain let go of its firm grip, freeing Violet from the worst of the anger.

"Well, now, I suppose you're right," Camilla said.

"Mom...can I come home to see you?"

"Of course. As soon as you can, okay? Or we'll come there if it'll be easier with your schedule—if that's okay with you?"

"You're welcome to visit anytime. But I'd like to come home." And maybe she'd admit to them she had stopped by recently but hadn't been ready to go in.

"That's wonderful, dear. Just call and let us know when."

"I'll call this week."

Movement caught Violet's eye. Jake was walking down the street toward her. "And, Mom, I'd like to bring someone special with me."

"A man?" she asked. "Would that happen to be your friend Jake West?"

"Yes," she said with a laugh. "A very special man."

Jake looked worried as he approached. He stopped, lifted her chin and searched the expression on her face. At his concern, love washed over her, making her smile.

His shoulders slumped in relief.

"We look forward to seeing you both," her mother said.

"Thanks, Mom. It was good talking with you."

When she ended the call, she rushed into his arms. "Oh, Jake…"

"Must've gone well," he said. "You look radiant."

She tilted her head back to look into his beautiful, dear eyes. "It was so simple. She apologized. I apologized. We're both relieved. Why didn't I return their calls sooner?"

"Because you were hurting. It's tough to be objective when the pain is so deep."

"And the guilt, wrapped up in anger, at them, at myself."

He gave her a gentle kiss, his soft lips brushing against hers. "I'm proud of you for calling them."

"Thanks, I feel…hopeful."

His eyes sparkled with the joy she felt. "Violet, I need to tell you—"

"Wait." She pressed her finger to his lips. "I need to finish first." She laughed at his look of surprise. "I told Mom I want to come visit and bring along someone special."

"Someone special?"

"I want you to meet my parents."

Frustration flashed on his face, but then it cleared. "I'll be happy to meet them."

"Are you sure? You don't look pleased."

"No, I'm good with it. When would you like to go?"

Disappointment over his reaction chipped away at her excitement. "Maybe Friday afternoon?"

"That should be fine."

She snaked her arms around his neck and leaned up on her toes. "Now, what were you about to tell me a minute ago before I interrupted?"

"Just that...well, that I'm glad this day turned out so well."

A bird in the tree above them chirped a happy song. She sighed. "It did, didn't it? I have a sense that everything will work out for the best."

He closed the gap and kissed her, making her knees go weak. She couldn't remember ever being happier.

But did he feel the same way she did? She wished he would say with words what she suspected he tried to say with his kisses.

Chapter Thirteen

The diamond engagement ring burned a hole in Jake's pocket.

He and Violet were going to drive three hours to South Carolina for him to meet Camilla and Buford Crenshaw. Meeting the parents, a first for him. But, more important, it would be Violet's family reunion.

A lot was resting on one visit.

Could he do this? Could he declare his feelings and propose as soon as Violet arrived at his house? Or should he wait until after meeting her mom and dad?

Her parents were society folks. Would Violet want him to be proper, to first ask her father for her hand in marriage?

Pacing the living room of his house, he ran a hand through his hair. She had said she wanted to take him home to meet her family. Maybe he should wait on the proposal. To make sure he met their approval.

What if they'd always dreamed of a doctor or lawyer for their daughter?

"Jake?" Violet called from the kitchen. "I'm here."

He froze, unsure. He didn't know anything about being a husband, being a *son-in-law*.

"Oh, there you are. What are you doing?" Violet asked.

She stood with the sunlight streaming over her short dark hair, her eyes bright…happy.

Calm settled over him. This amazing woman had been on her own for years. She was strong, capable, independent.

She didn't need her parents' permission to marry. And he didn't, either.

He might not know anything about being a husband or son-in-law, but he hadn't known anything about taking care of a baby, either. He could learn. Besides, he loved Violet and wanted to marry her. Nothing would change that.

"Jake?"

"You're beautiful."

A smile lit her face. "Thank you. Are you ready to go?"

"Not yet."

With a tilt of her head, she looked at him, questioning.

He stepped closer, ran a hand over her soft cheek. "I love you, Violet."

She blinked her gorgeous hazel eyes. A smile lifted the corners of her mouth. "I love you, too, Jake."

"Really?"

"Of course." She laughed and then gave him a soft kiss. "I don't babysit just anyone's niece, you know. I only do that for men I care about."

"Well, there won't be any other men to care about in your future. I'm it for you."

"Agreed." Joy shone in her eyes.

"So, does that mean you'll marry me?"

"You're asking?"

"Wait." Shaking his head, he stepped away from her. He needed to stay focused. "Having you so close made me forget all I had planned."

He pulled the ring from his pants pocket and held it in front of her, wishing he'd put it in a fancy box or had set up some kind of big surprise at a nice restaurant. "This was my mother's. I've kept it in my safety deposit box all these years. Never once considered taking it out. Until this past week."

"Oh, Jake. It's beautiful. Perfect. I'll treasure it."

"Violet Crenshaw, will you do me the honor of becoming my wife?"

She jumped into his arms and wrapped her arms around his neck. "Yes!"

He laughed as she almost knocked the ring out of his hand. She didn't care one whit how he presented it. She would have ripped through any wrapping anyway.

A big grin stretched across his face as he set her back on her feet and placed the ring safely on her finger. It was a little loose, but they could have it adjusted. "Do you mind that I didn't ask your parents' permission?"

"No. I'm thrilled and honored to introduce you to them as my fiancé."

He lifted her chin and touched his lips to hers. When she placed her hand on his chest and sighed, his heart pounded double time.

"I don't want a long engagement," he whispered.

"Me, either."

"Remy called today to say she's moving home right before school starts in August. Will you mind having her and Abby living with us for a while?"

"Not at all. I'll love having a baby in the house."

"And then maybe we can add one of our own?"

Pink tinged her cheeks. "I hope and pray."

He kissed her thoroughly and then forced himself to step away. "We need to leave. Time to meet the family."

She reached out and took his hand, and they walked out the door together.

"You're my family now, Jake."

He'd never been happier or more content in his life. Raising the back of her hand to his mouth, he kissed it. "I adore you. Together, we're going to build the family I've always dreamed of."

Epilogue

~~

"What's wrong with this thing?" Jake huffed as he gently tried to settle the infant car seat onto the base strapped in the backseat of the truck. "I think it's faulty."

"Jake, it's okay."

"How on earth are we going to get Camy home if they've sold us a bad carrier?"

Trying not to laugh at her husband, Violet stepped out of the wheelchair and thanked the nurse for bringing her outside. She placed a calming hand on Jake's arm. "Calm down, okay? You've done this before."

"But it's been two years since Abby was in one of the rear-facing s—" He stopped and shook his head, laughing at himself.

"Yeah, *rear-facing* is the key word here," she said, smiling at her precious, sleeping baby.

Camilla Lee West—Camy—slept peacefully through all Jake's efforts. Violet suspected with a dad as active as Jake, the child would learn to sleep soundly through just about anything.

With a head full of black hair, she looked just like Violet's baby pictures. But Violet could see her daddy in her, as well. Looked as if she would have his blue eyes.

He turned the seat the other direction and snapped it easily into place.

"See, even *you* can do it," she said with a teasing smirk.

"You're loving this, aren't you?"

"Reminds me of someone who once came roaring into my life with a backward car seat latched in by a tangled seat belt."

"Someone you instantly fell madly in love with, right?" He gave her a wink as he took her arm to help her up into the truck.

"Well, not instantly. But most definitely madly in love."

Violet had wanted to sit in the backseat next to Camy on the way home. She tucked the loose blanket over their baby's tiny feet.

"You're such a good mother," he said. "Are you doing okay?"

"I'm fine. Mom will arrive soon to help. And Remy and Abby are bringing dinner this evening. For now, I just want to get away from the chaos of the hospital to a quiet house with our girl."

"Our girl." He sighed, then leaned in and gave

her a long, leisurely kiss. "Too many nurses around to do that inside."

"And the patient drop-off area is so private," she said with a laugh, her cheeks burning.

"Let's go home, Mrs. West," he said, his dear face radiating love.

Home with her husband and daughter. She loved the sound of that.

* * * * *

Dear Reader,

Thank you for taking another journey with me to the fictional town of Appleton, Georgia. I hope you've enjoyed the story of Jake and Violet and baby Abby. I had such fun putting these two together to see what would happen. I also enjoyed revisiting some characters from my previous book, *The Guy Next Door*. I'm hoping you'll see one of those same characters again in a future story!

As I wrote this story, I thought I knew what my theme would be. But as happens sometimes, God leads the story in a different direction. What started out as a story about trying to earn love ended up being more about God taking all the junk in our lives and working it for good. And how sometimes, even though our lives may not turn out as we planned, we discover God blesses us with something even better.

Thank you so much for reading. I love hearing from readers. Please tell me what you think about *The Doctor's Second Chance*. You can visit my website, www.missytippens.com, or email me at missytippens@aol.com. If you don't have internet access, you can write to me c/o Love Inspired Books, 233 Broadway, Suite 1001, New York, NY 10279.

Missy Tippens

LARGER-PRINT BOOKS!

GET 2 FREE LARGER-PRINT NOVELS PLUS 2 FREE MYSTERY GIFTS

Love Inspired®

SUSPENSE
RIVETING INSPIRATIONAL ROMANCE

Larger-print novels are now available...